Woller

A NOVEL

Simon Marriott

A new idea seemed to be in circulation and on the rise as some of the existing ways of thinking were taking a fall of a topple gone sort. All of which was curious enough to those with a certain sense of their own known means who were eager to see how it would sink, slow on in, even to the most care free mind. And what might have been a slow realisation at first then became a sudden, urgent concern as the coming of a new idea sooner and not later was seen as the beginning of being either right or wrong. The surprise in the minds of those fennermarsh people who were quick enough to be so aware was that the words which had long been counted as missing were then reckoned to be more than much otherwise, closer than thought. What there was not, however, was a suggestion of how and when these could be used again which was a strange sort of notion to those who understood the consequences of forgetting. As a result of this, there were some who were hoping to find a new understanding through finking of an original sort, one of whom was Woller. As he looked at where his feet were standing and had stood, it occurred to Woller that he was less than more sure of whether to stand on the land or to stand in it or to sit on it or to sit in it. Some things seemed to be so and others did not which was rare enough explained. The where of his own two feet, leathered close in his shoes, was a flatter land than most which had earlier than then been the sea, the hardened edges being later on made as the water seeped through in a tidal creep to the softer fringes of reeds and sucking mud. With a searching thought, he wondered about the where of his own mattering means in a long before time, causing him to hold one of his arms level against his chest with the other arm being held just below his nose, in a measuring guess at how much of him would have then been under the brine with only the shine of a glare as an indication that a sack of bony someone might be in there, deep and soon to be gone. Such a thought caught a shivering hold on his bones, so he whacked a hand against the side of his head in an attempt to knock his brain onto a different thought. As he started to think about what the land might be, he quick time concluded that what it was in actual fact was flat and without expectation. The earth was scarred with dykes, long since dug which could be seen from the north to the south and from the east to the west, their essential presence ceasing to matter only on reaching the marshes on the edge of the Wash. At Gatt Beacon, one among numerous others, there was a constant moving, falling and rising, where earth turned to water, entering the channel through to Western Point, close by Herrion Sand and the mooring buoys, silent along Freiston Shore. A wilderness of water with a scarce remembered past, earlier than the earliest reckoned moments – a line of clodders, slodgers and yellow bellied hops. A land that ran at the call of the stationary engines which hummed to pump water wherever and whenever there was water to be pumped or to be sluiced, roaring through in a sounded crash of dirty white foam, down, out, then off around the channels and the cuts to the sea. As Woller leaned himself back as far as he could lean without falling over and down, he wondered at the how of the skies and their eye boggling size which seemed to a clod bound starer such as he was, raising a hand against the sun, to be without an ended top or a sided stop, weighted fast as they were onto the flat fields below. His wondering gaze held what he thought he recognised as an absence of need, of less than more of a care for the seeming urge of explanation or the anticipation of a huffed interpretation from elsewhere. And better than ever, he was of a mind to think this was a good way for it to be. What was harder for Woller to come to terms with was his confusion when attempting to mark either a recognised edge or a line of sight out in the fields, though, there was more than less of an ease in establishing a defining sense of place in the towns and communities that were scattered across the fen lands. Although, again, this could also be fraught due to a discernible lack of a vernacular stacking of bricks. There had, nonetheless, at some point, long time gone, been a large enough number of brick stacking attempts by those fennermarsh people who saw there was a need to raise whatever housing they could to cover over and in as many people as there were to be got inside, out of the flattening winds which tore in from over and across the eastern fen. At first, these communities were more than much rare and in no small way isolated until, slowly, each one increased in size and influence, encroaching on the surrounding settlements in which most of the fennermarsh people continued to live, even to the outer reaches of the fen lands. Over the mud to the sea, through the shallow creeks and around the sand bars interspersed with white salt flats in open water, sounded with the crying of geese. A calling to be heard from Fosdyke Wash to the Moulton Sluice. And then, the high old tide of the sea, coming in quick through the running creeks, under swinging ropes on the Langrick Ferry, reeds bending under wet slogged boots, over long cloddered earth, with the low hanging damp seen raised to the level of Gosberton Bank, though the channel through Dowdyke was long gone.

The finkers were encouraging in their ceaseless promotion of a central ideal. A single thread that ran like a sinew through the old systems of fennermarsh value which were then beginning to loosen and snap. There was much to be heard about the concerns of liberty in its various guises such as consciousness, the notion of the individual and the meaning of matter. Although long and more than less time before the unusual events at Pode Hole, such concerns were of not much interest to those who were thought to be questioning because it was accepted that a tension never failed to show between the autonomy of the individual and the consensus of the group. And it seemed to be a given that this was ever present, regardless of who was running the show. As for the fennermarsh people themselves, the breathing of liberty had long time allowed them to choose the how and the when and the where and the why that they were, while each of them talked and wanted and loved and hurt and acted or abstained. The themes which dominated the condition of thumbed opposition were not only pinned down at the beginning of being, they were also rooted in choice and the way in which they chose to construct the rules by which they might live. The erosion of such themes by means of barely noticeable controlling acts caused a late awareness about that which was underpinned, with the understanding that it could also be undermined. As a consequence of this massing of opinion, the seeping, creeping of scatter flown tales for both the new way and the older ways of the fennermarsh people became more than less apparent. The idealism of the finkers had initially reflected this with a united keening voice which was concerned with everything and with nothing, each of which was accorded equal importance. But so close as it was to real recent time events, with the accepted and the usual becoming less than acceptable and more than unusual, their words had taken a sudden turning over to an urgent tone. It was then a surprise even to him, when, on setting it out in an easy to hear manner of talking words it was the curious Amos Cloot who came to be the first to mention a possible encounter of his own with the meedler vong. What could be thought of as less than surprising was that from the exact moment of his first mentioning it, the possible and the arguable whereabouts of the meedler vong sank like a virus into the brain of those with wont enough for the sinking. And sudden time soon, when it was sunk down and in as far as was needed which was almost as much as might have been thought, the spiralling of the viral code kicked on in, hooking the carrier with a bursting thirst for the whatever news of the meedler vong they could get. With no hint of a warning, the carrying came on quick then passed on and pushed out with chattering words moving and shaking with practiced ease, a constant source of fascination on the inside of a distracted head. Those who were fond of the right and the wrong were eager to curtail the spreading of curious thought even though none of them knew where or from whom the curious thinking had come. What *was* known by the fennermarsh people themselves was that those who could do so would find ways of knowing in order to turn what seemed to be a mere given chance into a halting conclusion, enough to scupper the use of quick running legs. Whenever it was taken, each endorsed action was effective in bringing about a desired way of thinking, even among most of those who were scattered throughout the wider fen lands only with the added complication that this included some of those minds which would have been better not to be affected, sat plump as they were in the heads of the finkers of the cultural elites. It was this which raised a chatter of surprise with the shovellers in the spoongrease dinner shops, precisely because the one individual who had gone to the bother of taking a rummage around on the inside of his own mind in the vaguest of hopes he might pull out something of interest had indeed been the curious Amos Cloot, doing what no one else had thought to do about the evident happening of events. And succeeding, as he did so, in throwing aside the covers of those who were responsible for their actions. At the same time, he had made it clear and understood that there appeared to be more to be known than had ever been supposed on the notion of a lining up between the meaning and the meant and the changing shape of things. But even though Amos Cloot had found a new way of understanding the mattering means which would be different to what was and had always been the way things were, it was an odder thing still that not even he or another single finking individual or even a maddening crowd could be found to give a reason of the why and the how and the when it had happened.

It was around this time of mounting, shape induced blankness that Woller first turned himself up in the remaining thoughts of those in the western fen, when he decided to start on in with a question of his own about such a peculiarly random abandonment of finking convention and the question he asked was, why not? Such words as why and not, when put together as Woller had done, were considered to be big small words by the finking elites and once each had been uttered they caused a new outbreak of large scale pondering in the minds of those who were mostly minded to lie down on the ground or attempt to forget. It was in this manner that Woller inadvertently announced his own curious self at the time of his arrival in Gosberton Clough which was the place of all places that was then a more than less important part of his happen done ways, at least for the time that it was. On the day that he had first wandered through and around the barely more than a few streets of Gosberton Clough, Woller had not so much decided on doing but rather, with a quickening flash, had leapt his own self straight up and knocked with a knuckled hand on the outside of a door in the side of a house that he not seen before. And one which he was quite without knowing exactly what was on the other side. Although he was reckoned on it being not only a door but on it being *the* door on which he needed to be knocking. It was, however, not something he could explain he was minded to think. Stood where he was out in the street, at the side of the house and looking at the door which was painted an eye blinking shade of lime green, he was pleased to think of himself as not much surprised when it was opened by a woman in a tart yellow dress who seemed to be wearing nothing on her feet yet at the same time pretending to wear something by means of a rough outline of a shoe drawn in ink on each of her bare feet. A woman who introduced herself only as the woman who owned the house. Ushering him through to the inside, she showed Woller to the top of the stairs on the second floor where there was a room she said he might like to see while he was there. As he looked at the room, he could see that it was somewhat bare apart from a single metal framed bed placed against one wall and a white plastic chair which was tipped over on its side on the smooth wooden floorboards in the middle of the room. Ha hum, he thought to himself. But then he reckoned that the look of the place was not the sell of it for him as much as the quiet and the clear absence of any keeling smells which he decided was a good thing. And so with the nodded approval of the woman who owned the house he agreed to cash up her account and move himself in. He was less than more sure of how well knowing the woman in the tart yellow dress and inked feet who owned the house was that the room had been vacant for reasons which were obvious enough, as she did not appear to change her expression from one of hope to one of relief when he telling told her that he would take the room. Although, he thought he caught a hint of a smile at the corners of her mouth as she handed him the key to his door before wandering back down the stairs to wherever it was in the house she had been earlier than then. Alone with his own self for a moment, Woller stared at the tipped over chair lying on the floor with what appeared to be a reasoning lack even though it occurred to him that it might have been put where it had in a deliberate way. Hum ha, he thought, as he reached out a hand to turn it back on its standing legs. With his sense of balance restored, he walked over to the small window that was set low into the wall opposite the bed and which he saw, as he leaned close to the pane, overlooked a large apple tree but not much more except whatever could be seen through the stripped winter branches which were thick about the outside wall of the house; almost within touching distance of where he was stood, on his toes and with a cheek pressed against the glass in the hope of seeing to one side. Still standing, he was sudden time caught with a keeling need to ease his long boned self onto the metal framed bed. And so he did. Waking early, as a pale dappling of light was thrown across the room through the small, low set window, Woller was caught in the brain with a sudden realisation that it was the morning of the first day in January. A day on which he had agreed, in keeping with the recent time arrangement with Shepeau Stow to start on in as a new come finker, allowed to be there, as he was, as a help doing means to an end even though he was less than more sure what this might entail. But then caring little for the whatever and the however of the arranging as it had been done by whoever had been keen to be doing it, he was out of the metal framed bed and pushing his arms and his legs into his sweater and his trousers, as he snatched up his coat from the white plastic chair. And shoving his feet hard in his shoes, he tumbled himself in a flight down the stairs from the second floor and out through the lime green painted door in the side of the house to the street. Pulling a breather of the crisp air deep in through his nostrils as he walked, he could feel a sense of pleasing warmth spreading about his loose hanging bones with the realisation that it was without doubt the month of January he was then in, well knowing as he was that if a lined out and numbered space on a calendar could ever have been made to measure, then it was measured up close in a good size for him. This was contrary to the broke shouldered staggering of his friends and those who knew him, for whom the month pitched a sense of a sort more halting than it was moving. Woller was minded to think that he had been given a go to be free to associate in a way that only a fresh come, new beginning would allow. Which meant that with January holding no measure to be sought, he returned the favour by accepting such grace as well as he could. And with his own self occupying the space vacated by the

weight of expectation through the virtue of simply being who
he was. He was reckoned too on one other reason he thought
of as in no way small shaped, which was that from the start to
the end, the month was fen stark and cold. This, he knew to be
a good thing, with colder being better than warmer, offering
him, as it did, fewer moments to be scared up frit about smells
of the keeling variety. Woller stretched out a smile from the
corners of his mouth and clutching his wrapping tight around
his bones he wandered off to see who or what he might find.
Those who lived in and around Gosberton Clough gave the
appearance of having recovered well from the shock of the
unusual events at Pode Hole. And for most of them but
without much of a surprise not for all of them in the various
finking groups to have experienced it, the transition between
the unusual events at Pode Hole and the period subsequent to
such a momentous happening as it had been, had loosed off a
series of episodes which amounted to an outcome of a positive
and a progressive time. Being, as he was, a new come learner of
finking ways with a need to understand as much as he could
about the mattering means, Woller was minded to think he
ought to make an effort to record in a noted book of scrawl
what he saw as the end of the hiatus of the previous month,
what he imagined to be the beginning of a soon to happen time.
And though he was not then allowed to participate directly in
the mattering means of the various members and associates of
the Gosberton Clough cultural elite, he continued to scrawl
down words nonetheless as he wrote of the peculiarly wailed
nostalgia that more people than a few had begun to feel for a
just gone time. But as blue eyed Basil was keen to say to his
friends and those who knew him, all this of course was in
retrospect, knowing, as each and all did that in actual fact or in
various different facts with variable factors and in varying
truths, at the time of the events themselves an overarching sense

of despair had been adopted as the prevailing emotion. Which soon time and enough had leaked straight through to the broader set thoughts of all those fennermarsh people who were scattered throughout the wider fen lands and amongst whom a certain vogue became attached to the loose hauled development of personal clattering. There was a point of view almost commonly held by all but one of the poorly head shrinkers who were known for their views on such things that this could be ascribed to unresolved issues arising from an exposure to the excitement of the unusual events at Pode Hole. This was something of a surprise because no small number of those who then affected to cultivate their clattering talents had none of the down on the spot, personal experience of what exactly had happened at Pode Hole. At least, none that would have thrown them a qualifying chance at the clattered bawl each of them seemed so desperate to do. Another thing the clatterers had not anticipated was their being pinned down as a particular factor in the seeming fashionability of strident negativity which had become a relevant matter to be talked about, when the first scrawlings in Wollers notebooks were eventually brought to the attention of those who were more attentive than otherwise. Among the freedoms which were almost inevitably lost in circumstances such as those which arose in the case of whoever might be of a scowling persuasion, was the taken liberty to be despairing about the future. To be despairing about the belligerent happening of things that affected those who could least afford to be affected by them. To be despairing of the human race itself and what they considered to be its racing inhumanity. The weight of pessimism had become a sort of betrayal of the supposed norm and a curious, compulsory optimism was expected to prevail because for as long as the fennermarsh people could remember, anything and everything that had appeared in the pressing rags had been haw hawingly accompanied by the obligatory and the dazzlingly optimistic prognoses of the eventual outcome. A common occurrence was that even large scale reversals and the occasional catastrophe of a collapse in understanding of that which needed to be understood, by those were encouraged to understand, were to be packaged with a shine and given out clean as part of a general strategy of well conceived brilliance in the art of telling things as they ought to be told. There were some who recognised that it was desirable to suggest that in the period subsequent to the unusual events at Pode Hole, a number of sanctioned reforms would need to be found. Measures that could ensure the fennermarsh people were offered a measure of their own cashed up prosperity, a chance for all of easy bought justice, of smile stretching happiness and the freedom to be who they were. And even who they wanted to be. It was seen that there was a need for the fennermarsh people to be given at least the wave handed opportunity to believe in such ideals and also proffered the chance of a pursuit of whatever it was each of them thought to be more important than otherwise; some of them, sometimes not wanting to see that it was a proffering of much less than more. And in a paradox with bite, it had to be insisted over and again that if as a consequence of restoring a balance between the mattering means and the occasional averting of catastrophe, so many individuals were to be lost, then maybe the notion of individuality itself was one not worth having. As a weight of strained enthusiasm, it was a harder thing than thought to fake the wanted reaction for most of the fennermarsh people, not least for the finkers who considered themselves to be vulnerable to the positive faking which had to be expressed with a familiar ease without seeming to be borrowed from elsewhere. The finkers of the Gosberton Clough cultural elite were as one in their resolve to make no exceptions among themselves in the process of adaptation. And when it was reckoned to be a necessity, each of them, together and in turn, were plain and straight in their attitude to the fakers game. While their collective reasoning was levelled at the vogue for such new raised documents as the Vermuyden Charter which had been at the height of its popularity before the unusual events at Pode Hole. The result of such strange words and actions was a keening need in some minds for the sincere, along with a growing interest in the honourable, run through as it was with a contempt for quick boled hype. Among the finkers, there was a realisation that they could not and that they ought not to allow themselves to be fooled by well wrought sentiments of a seductive sort, as for whom so ever had been most affected in the weeks after the unusual events at Pode Hole, it had not been a question of starting again but of something more than less fundamental and harder to do which was to begin from the beginning itself. There was, however, a reluctance to simply return to the ceaseless hauling of matter from which they had attempted to take themselves clear and it was this which when made real in a welter of collective confusion, gave the days, in spite of the cold, a misleading appearance of booze sunk abandon. At the same time, there was in the concerned minds of each and all of the finkers a recognition that a meaning of some sort could be implemented in a quiet enough scheme, in as finking a manner as was possible in the circumstances. The almost unanimously arrived at conclusion called for the continued interrogation of the mattering means and the continual investigation of ideals both real and imagined, broken in the cause of idealistic stumbling which it was mostly agreed by most of those who were involved was a needed release. At the same time too, there were some amongst the fennermarsh people who were eager to be wider known for something other than their own marsh cloddered nous, with this being reckoned to matter less and not more than a clattering go of mattering means, much in the same vein as the investigations of the finkers. There were others still who were keen to be seen to be cured of the manners which had pulled in no small number of dawdlers along in their wake to be felled with a falling crack, down and headed on quick to the extended wobble in fortunes which therefore meant it was an easier thing than could have been thought to suggest that convention must be challenged there and then. In the opinion of those who had one to offer and who usually did, a degree of earlier before hung around and weighted down peg taking had been the cause for whatever actions were indeed taken. Woller was minded to keep on going in whatever direction it was that he was headed because it seemed to him to be the only way in which he could continue with the least sense of confusion, knowing as he did that whatever balance he then had might take a keeling blow if he were to stumble off in a clatter which was not of his own doing. And besides, he decided that a direction of an obvious sort would only pin down that which was certain and at such a noo wah suggestion he took a head churning lurch and wound up his feet for a falling crash. On the matter of doing what he did with as much of his own self made mind as he could, Woller was caught with a thought that had caused him to ponder on the how and the why and the when of his earlier started involvement with the more established finkers, occurring to him, as it did that a possible moment of joining significance had been a mention he had made of a piece in his own scrawled hand on the need for a finker to be at the centre of somewhere, where something was happening, wherever and whatever that was. But when he tried to recall the happened done matter in more detail than less, he wondered if he had been aware at the time that those listeners who were there, who had taken the bother to come in and sit with as small a fidgeting scratch as they could, were buttoned right down with a hang on each of his spoken words. And so, it was less than more of a surprise that his work which had also been whacked with a start at a critical time and crashed in on with boots and with fists on the ends of flailing arms and kicking legs as well as shouted words and rotten scrawls, had sudden time quick become a cause for celebration. Although whether or not the means taken on to get where he had got were a call for a ha hum sigh or a hum ha frown, he was further off knowing for sure than before. Sooner rather than later, however, he moved on with wanting to know about much of the recent time happening of how it was the finkers were minded to reach for pushing the notion of daring to its absolute limit whatever this might be, with the conclusion being drawn that the absolute limit of daring was not to be found in the furthest reaches of clapped out hope but that it was more nuanced than might have been thought – with an appearance in opposition to how it was seen. At the same time, it was known that there were some of a finking lean who were keen on the hand raised notion of suggesting such a limit as being either one of abstention or a move to remove the mattering means, ending in a sudden come silence. As seemed to be usual with Woller, another thought then threw his mind over to a curious look at a crack in his own known learning, with his reckoning on this being that just as the limit of daring could be found in silence, then, by the same token, real own knowing could be pinned on acceptance rather than a removal of means. And while he was less than more sure of just how well known something ought to be thought, he knew well enough that much the same as an odd hung smell, a permanent removal of means also seemed to be much in the air as a result of an attempt at fomenting whatever form of running protest could be fomented in Walpole by the finkers who were there on the spot. With a quick scratched plan in their heads they had made use of a curling mark as a trigger for action which even though action was not something that was seen to happen, the meaning well of the affair produced a question to be asked which was, could sudden gone matter be a solution to a no found reason for losing heads or burning out, with no needing to be or of nothing to be had? To the big time surprise of almost all those who heard it the answer to this question, from almost all those who voiced it, was no. There was, nonetheless, the occasional exception when some flamboyant fennermarsher or other had taken it on themselves to make a removing go of the mattering means in a crowd entertaining manner. Although, for some, this was closer to a reeling show than it was to a tragedy because for those finkers who were eager to establish a line of their own, a removal of sorts was not only a well wrought ideal, it was an actual choice to be made. And sooner than expected, it was seen to be so when without much of a mention, a curator who had founded an archive for fennermarsh thought and who had also been a forger of the Gosberton Clough cultural elite, took his own means in a one shot take. As far as some of the new come finkers were concerned, however, the more than otherwise intriguing case of a once taken shot was seen as futile gesture by someone who seemed to exist as much in the ether and in the imagination of those who existed only through their work. But in spite of being a man lost to silence, the curator had, nevertheless, done all he could to complete a memory against forgetting with his ending reached ahead of the obvious conclusion that of the archive he produced, there survived fewer than more of the memories he had collected in his own shortened time. As a consequence of this, there were finkers who felt compelled to make it explicit in their scrawled down words that after more than less considered time, after a rubbing of chins and a tearing of hair, there were fewer reasons than could be thought for continuing on with meaning or matter without a change for the better of some sort of other. As no more were there reasons to be found for departing too soon with a well heard crack. One which would be all the more noisily discussed in hurling words. What there was, after all of the rubbing of chins and the tearing of hair, was a collective lean to a leaving well alone of whichever choice could be made. A realisation that even though much could be lost when some were cut loose from finking notions, there was no better notion to be sought, caught the finkers with relief, not least because the confusion which could be earlier heard in their argued words was not made so apparent as to have become an open gawper of fretted hand wringing to be better avoided by whom so ever could do so. Woller too was curious about the mattering means. And the how and the what of a life well lived through, as opposed to the vexed complication of leaving it, the latter being a sentiment which he saw as an encouragement to continue on with the will never to be caught, lost in a frowning grump. On the follow of a seen easy nonchalance, the growing impression amongst those who were on the outside of the fink was that there was a slow coming together of former competing sorts who were earlier thought to be mutually exclusive. While at the same time, there was also, in some quarters which were different again, an idealism to he heard in the spoken words that in spite of this each and all were made of the same handed weave, cleaved and caught tight in the fabric of the other. And for others looking on from somewhere that was elsewhere, it had become obvious enough that with an appropriately persuasive hand the fennermarsh people would take to a given out way of being with more of a keening need than otherwise could be found among those who were considered to be well assured of their own purpose. Much of this was due to an expectation which sat at a slight angle, tipped over and topple gone in the glare of events as they were. And most being only part formed, as much of it could be. Although, seeing as how there was merely the beginning of an assertion to such claims, it was assumed by some that just such a popular attitude had earlier been a starter for the attempted development of a personally held individual notion of own known means throughout the fen lands at their widest and at their longest. It was, therefore, balanced in some minds, finking and otherwise, as a not bad happened thing, along with a continuing curiosity in whatever could be learned from the hurtling, endless search for knowledge. In addition to this, there was a further widening of interest in the whereabouts of the meedler vong with even the search itself fast becoming news – a development which bounced a reflection back from a collective pouring out and pulling in of need. Amongst the finkers, it was reckoned that there were those of a frowning sensibility who were not cowed or stuck down fast as elements of a slugged conservatism scattered across the various whereabouts of the flat lands. More to the point, they were capable of speaking their own words with other louder boomed voices on matters which they considered to be of some importance such as the supposed end of the period of well fashioned, elegant scepticism opposed to a reasoning lack, over which they had watched until it seemed to have reached a point long way gone where all were agreed on the need for a conclusion of sorts. There were others who were thought to be caught with a lock of a hold in what some suspected was a wrong headed search for identity. One which could only be of value to the finkers who were concerned that the notion of integrity would be presented as a common seen factor in all finking processes, leaving them with nothing more than a brain cracking course of action. And so with an absence of something to hurl their words against, those who were left with less than much at all were concerned about the prospect of falling back down to wallow in a warming gloop of sincerity.

Understanding this well enough, it was a wide minded thought that such concern could easily turn to alarm. This was considered to be a bad thing. There would then be a keening need for the services of a number of finkers who could be encouraged to accept connecting roles in order to provide a buffering stop against the coming of the barging charge, with the essential point being to pin down the approval of those who had composed what had come to be known, only as the most recent elements in a process of never otherwise mentioned innovation. As a consequence, there was an understanding that while some things could not be categorised, they could, nonetheless, be sanctioned with no concessions to eloquent explanation. Some of those who had considered the matter for some time were close on wondering whether there ought to be a limiting hold on any sanctioning actions as it was reckoned that this was even more than less vital than it ever had been, earlier than then, as there was much to be done in order to protect and maintain even the most basic of free notions which seemed to be slowly disappearing without consent. Those who spoke the fennermarsh tongue were keen to lay down their own rules, even though their interests were less a matter of reason than a consequence of the sympathies and antipathies which grew out of them. Opinions could easily enough become well established as a frame of reference for those of a morally persuaded sort, secure and resolute, as each and all of them were in their own confident recognition of whichever thoughts and actions were deemed to be worth sanctioning. And as such, it was no small surprise that it sooner and not later became a topic of much spoken debate – some of it quieter than might have been hoped for, by those with a need for fennermarsh thought.

The intersection of fink and a mubbelling lug encouraged among some, a kind of fawning over the shine of bright, hard won ideals which to a larger than lesser extent had already begun to seep, low and slow through cracked and vulnerable bones, to govern the responses of even the usually well shod, lockers of local values. Almost all of which had been a long time held, only to be a short time gone. In the quick springing minds of those who were involved, a charismatic individual was needed to throw out a line of dependable reassurance to all those of a wobbling touch that the finkers of both the Tydd Gote and Gosberton Clough cultural elites were equal to the task of catching on and fastening down the valuable matter. At least, before, there was none left to be taken or none to be lost. It was, therefore, agreed that approaches were to be made to blue eyed Basil. This was reckoned to be more hopeful than otherwise as while on the one hand, blue eyed Basil was aware of the har de har, the scared frit visions and portraits of the situation they were in, he was less than keen to lose a sense of his own balance when measuring it against the values of a welcoming smile. There was a finking disappointment when he declined to take up the offer, choosing to throw it back in rather than out. One of the consequences of this was that some finkers then decided to take on the line themselves in an attempt to push at what they saw as the rough scouring of the fen lands, as, almost without exception, the fennermarsh people and the finkers were agreed on the significance of the more than before relevance to the means of self owned living. And for the finking juice, for the entertaining berserkers and the hair pulling, tongue sticking ranters too, it was thought that with the action of pushing out their new lines of reckoning, the earlier hurled words were ham crackered down and moved out of sight. It then came as a big size surprise to all those who were looking on close with an interest of their own, how some of the earlier chucked finkers were stood somewhat outside of this celebration of enthusiasm, consumed, as they seemed to be, by their own frantic attempts to pull in a combined showing of the recognised finking brains. And at the first suggestion of the thing, these finking brains seemed to have given them a nodded approval to reach an accord with the smarter, tarter theorists, involved in a hum ha ponder on the causes of the way things were. Struck worse with gloom, each of them eventually saw that a few more than not of their hurled out bawlers, following on with a gathering weight of their earlier gone actions had caused the offending of some with their own thinking lack at what they were convinced, in a shared reckoning, was a boiler of fat gorged celebrity and vulgar publicity as much as a gesture toward the new come establishment. It would then, sooner than snap, happen for something to provoke those who were frequently known to be concerned by that which almost never concerned them. Those, who now began to contrive a growing anger over what they saw as the open scorning of a loss of understatement. And not least, the long abandoned search for the certainty of the right and not the wrong thing. The dog eared gurning of others with a well worn line in mocking words, served only to show how slow they were to realise that their behaviour had set them apart from the rest and brought them to the attention of those who were known to always be right. There were some who held the opinion that it was because of this that more finkers than not began to demonstrate a complete lack of interest in the need to make what were, nonetheless, agreed to be, fevered, cheapening statements, even though the continual threat of conflict made for a potential rise in the process of radicalisation. And following this, the polarisation of ideas and ideals. From the start, it seemed to be obvious enough that a manner of smack minded bone cracking had been one of the first to be used weapons in the hands of some who were quick to scowl at the slightest provocation, either from the least speaking shufflers or the most radical berserkers. It was when the hack scribblers first published the words and pictures of Silvester Guillory who had only just before, gone clattering into a prominent member of the loose collective from Amber Hill that Woller realised in his own mind how far the colouring of reason in previously reasonable minds, had been caused to advance. And he wondered whether or not other finkers besides him had been kicked in the brain with the same realisation or had simply been towed under by the pull of the prevailing sensibilities, especially on hearing rumoured second handed chatter. As often seemed to be the how of it, he was less than more sure again when he heard that the street bawled words accusing some publications of being not what they were, were as a result of them being turned over as forums not for information itself but for the disinformation, the misinformation and the informing of those whose thoughts had been previously formed. Then later than could have been sooner, the appearance of a manifesto calling for action caused no small confusion in finking minds with a widening crack leading on into in a shouter of division, as most of them were off too fast and hurtling quick, crashing, colliding and falling, dazed with the effort of tearing down high raised words in a maddening rush. Stranger still, it seemed to Woller, looking on as he was, when Cornelius Karp then sat up and announced in a sudden flash of turning speed that he would offer his support to Silvester Guillory for whichever course of action he might be keening to take. One group who were known to almost all of the fennermarsh people were the yellow bellies. And even these peculiar individuals, who were often to be found somewhere that was elsewhere, wrapped tight in their own reckoning of safe hiding, were caught with a bewildering scratch of their own minded thoughts before remembering the yellow bellied conviction that through the use of their own particular methods, they alone had succeeded in remaining away from and therefore, less than most affected by the recent time events which had knocked into the bones of everyone but them. It was understood with a confusing smile for some that those who would be yellow of belly were scattered throughout the fens to the east and to the west and to the north and to the south and would, in most senses of the ordinary, have drawn in much less than little attention to themselves if it were not for their occasional need to see nothing. During times of stressed out heaving and hurled out stressing of a far from reasonable sort, the yellow bellied ones would place their collective faith in covering their eyes, in each of their own heads, with their hands, in an attempt to shut out whatever was happening on the outside of the fast covered brain. It could be seen that those who were caught by surprise in a sudden quick go of a terror frit shriek would make for a home made hide with a wrist snapped action, flashed through with astonishing speed of such and so much that it had to be done wherever and whenever each or all of them might be. As a result of their speeded reactions, the yellow bellies were often to be seen either one at a time as a sole standing figure, stilled in a street or clustered together in small numbered groups, stood to their knees out in the green blades of a sweet grassed meadow. At other times, they could be seen to be felled on their backs and laid out in shock, down on the ground from a quiet slipped shoe to a loud cracked top or clattering about in a boozer or a spoongrease dinner shop, spilling booze onto collars and tipping grease over sleeves, as none of them much were able to see or to know any which way as to how each one of them might go. Worse would then come from looking as they did, when, noodled and lost, some yellow bellies could land in the hands of those with a har de har har laugh who clonked them with sticks and who rattled them with stones, who drew on their heads and who kicked at their bones. Birds flapped down from above to search for a perch and dogs howled their ears back at the sight. And for some of the people who were right and not wrong, the yellow bellies were only waiting to be collected while they were each and most of them still in the dark.

It had become apparent, to his friends and those who knew him that in spite of what he was supposed to be doing, even if that which he had taken notice of was taken into account, much of what had been going on and happening around him (the mattering means of almost everyone else) had more than less completely passed Woller by. They decided amongst themselves on there being three distinct reasons for the how and the why of his merely glancing encounters with the sound and the touch of people other than his own self during all of those hours when he was awake to the wider fen lands. The first point on which agreement was reached was his remarkable absence, his near total lacking of a smartening manner, as observed by those who cared about such things. And by those who cared about what was thought of them, in the opinion of whoever it was they considered to be worth taking suggestions from. Woller was thought to be filled up to his brimming top with an elegant bearing all of his own but not one which had been instructed or bellowed in on him from outside his own brain. The second point being that he was reckoned to be not so intentionally but nonetheless and in particular, better than good at allowing trouble to pass him by without stopping, not troubling trouble unless trouble troubled him. A third and final point to be made on his behalf, by his friends and those who him, was that in spite of his close, own learned knowledge of the fennermarsh people and the recognised on the spot finking brains which were there to be found, he was drawn with a quickening immediacy straight on in to the circle of finkers who surrounded Silvester Guillory who offered without a hitch, a more rational and restrained way of things getting done.

The wider reputation of the finkers throughout the fen lands, the opportunities afforded to a curious individual by the various finking movements and the thirsting pull of places such as Tydd Gote, Gosberton Clough and Wisbech were, each and all, big time decided factors in the trailing in of the enquiring and the hankering and the grasping and the grappling, much coming numbers of new come migrants, come from wherever it was they had been before then. It had been an obvious enough assumption to make, among those who were less than more sure that a person with the calling of a finker would thrive on a reluctance to become attached to any form of conclusive wagging of a mardy old dog and a barker of slogans of the right and the wrong. Although, through the use of a method of label pinning in the words of the scowling kind, there was an inadvertent bodging together of one type of sorted category of finker which was then employed to throw a contrasting glare against another, the other finking sort. Still, it seemed, even with the apparent staking out of fastened positions that a done happened element of finking slippage was to be seen in spite of the efforts of those squealers who considered the effort to be a good thing. And who were pleased with a distinction being drawn between creative minds and a larger number who sought an excess of fame and success; those who were snatching hard in achievement while raking the proceeds through their fingers in a snorted appreciation of a moodled, over boodled, less than more filling way to be on the inside of the own known self. And somewhere that was elsewhere, wherever it was at the time, others who could be found among the down to the bones radical finkers and the charging bargers who were content to be as much themselves as not without need of apology or of responsibility or of whatever form of explanation might be expected. Unless it was of their own choosing that is. Such finkers were reckoned by occasional scrawlers to be applauded by their own, self same hands, with an appreciation, a feeling that to be a creative brain and a finker were one and the same thing. It was also a common finking experience to have felt a connection with the fennermarsh people, for them to be a counter to those who were always right rather than wrong. And it was even accepted to be counted on for a support that was given out free, with the understanding of it being something which could not and did not have to be bought. Because this situation was the making of a secure held context in which any sharp keen fennermarsher who would be a finker could develop and advance their own ideas, it was one that was not much to be liked by those who considered themselves to be of the sort who might not approve. Woller, however, had become easily knowing of the possibilities on offer to his brain almost immediately on arriving in Gosberton Clough, though he had also realised that wherever things were possible, by the same token, they could also be problematic. Ha hum, he thought, ha mubbelling hum, before pausing for a moment to quieten his own self with a question. The humming and haa-ing of which was where he would go now.

The School of Thought was attached to Ayscoughfee Hall. The location of which had the effect of lending the bricks of the place a much wanted superior touch. And even with a consideration held out to the collectors of other collections of a similar reckoning or to whichever related organisations were of an equal standing, to be sent to there was a wanted thing, a thing to be had among those who had only that. A shorter distance than it looked from the School of Thought, attached to Ayscoughfee Hall, were three smaller schools which had also been established on the order of minds being learned. In addition, each of these had been charged with the function of feeding the larger school with the better than most and the brightest of their students; all of whom were then filled using the same method of filling a brain as had always been used. A method, it was hoped by some which would remain in use. Such a way of learning being done was not a public seen thing but instead was reserved as a private matter for those on the inside rather than the outside, even though it had never been explained why and was, therefore, expected to be accepted as it was. On walking through the main front doors of the hall and under the worded lintel which sat, fat, over a craning head, the sight of a coming through learner, of either the giving or the taking sort, was barged in on by the chisel scrawled telling of how and when it was those of a learning sort had decided to encourage the doors to be swung open and not closed, as they might otherwise have preferred them to be. And it was this, from his first ambled leg through (and under) and for each of the times after that which Woller found to be the cause of a gentle smile which would begin to stretch out from the corners of his mouth. Holding down such a look, he was minded to wonder at the seeming innocence on display. And he knew that even those who had little or no big time interest in being interested in that which was interesting to him, would know that the school owed the continuation of its open doors to the period of confusion that had marked the latter stages of the unusual events at Pode Hole as much as to those learning types who were harder than pressed to reach a decision of whatever sort. In part, this was due to no small amount of squabbling between themselves at the time, being, as it was, a period that knocked a shape into the values and the institutions which were largely to dominate the well worn schemes of each and all of the fennermarsh people who had been scattered throughout the wider regions, for longer than most of them would have imagined. There were those of a finking persuasion who had heaped worded praise on the magnificence of the hall as it looked from the outside, not simply because they thought it stood better from without than from within but because that was where it felt more than could have been comfortable, in the circumstances. In his own way, this looking in from without rather than looking out from within or even around from within, caught Woller in the brain as a quite bonkers method of choosing to think what was to be thought about a matter, especially in the cause of a reckoned ideal to be made. Although even then he was never quite sure how a reckoned ideal was understood to have been reached, by whom so ever might have wanted to do so. He was, nevertheless, well seeing and appreciative of the far older than he was, stone flagged floors and the dark varnished wood of the panelling which clung to the walls from the skirted boards to a height three quarters of the way up, almost to the top of the sharp turning staircases of which there were three on the ground floor. Of these, there were two that were in use. And as such, could be ascended and descended in a usual manner. While the third seemed to be a staircase more hopeful than otherwise, running, as it did, from a footed level, down and then up again in a loop before returning a curious stepper to somewhere close to where they had started. Woller knew, somehow that this in combination with the air of learned thoughtfulness with which the people on the inside went about their thoughtful learning, would have been a reflection and a confirmation of what Cornelius Karp had already said if only he could remember what it was Cornelius Karp had been saying at the time when he did. With nothing to be done, he was stuck only with forgetting. And even as he tried to imagine the worded sounds of his voice at the time, he could not pin it down with any recognised ease. So he decided on making it up instead, as he turned over in his own mind a quietened down speech, lining out the necessity of a competitive, well schooled performance in a well performing schooling. And though he could not explain this even to his own brain, he thought that it sounded as he expected it would. Also, he was vaguely aware of something that someone else had either talking told him or that he had seen written in a scrawled hand along the seemingly reasonable line that to be a recognised hangeronner and a respecter of the supposedly respectable done mattering means of those who were schooled with an agenda of their own, with an interest in keeping it so, would make a degree of personal influence a shored up and much needed certainty. Whether or not this was a good or a bad thing caused a deep harring hum between his ears. In addition to it being a serious place where matters such as swoondling were taken as keen to be discussed by the students without the insistent pressure of their being put in a position to do so, by anyone other than themselves, it occurred to Woller that a stretching thread of ideas and solutions to the complications of various big weighted questions had been pulled. And it was still maintaining a pull with a tightening grip on the need to be of a curious mind, though not only in terms of a shake. As a consequence, he made a note in his own handed scrawl to be appropriately curious as much as he could.

One of the first things to catch a hold of his attention on the day he turned himself up there was how immediately apparent it was that there were no students to be seen or to be heard or even to be considered. What was not so obvious to Woller and was harder to be known about, not just for him, was that an explanation for this peopled lack was the introduction of a small but effective spanner thrown token of well assured prejudice. One which had earlier been sanctioned by those who were of the nodded opinion that it was an idea better than it was not, even though some of them had been confused as to exactly what such a not might be. Worse than this, there seemed to be no way to talk this over with anyone else because the words which were needed to do that seemed to be missing from the book of well endorsed vernacular, with no trace of where and when it had gone. In and around both the school itself and among the students who were registered as being allowed to be there, an atmosphere of well sat, well stood, well walked, well thought, well said and well done, extended from the minded to the physical. In particular, to the handed touch and the boggling gog of each given but less than barely accommodating apartment. These were listed in the educational files of the school as being for the sleeping there of the researchers, of which Woller had recent time become one. That the apartment in which he was then standing was the one in which he ought to be doing so, Woller was less than he could have been sure, as he had been left on his own to find it from the moment he had pushed open the main front doors of the hall to walk through and in without even so much as a basic telling of where it might be. The apartment that he supposed ought to be his and in which he was now stood, presented him with an immediate concern of wondering about whatever it seemed to be that he could smell. And whether or not it could be smelled only by him. As such, it would then either be not there at all or worse than that it might be faint but dangerous, being detectable by no one else other than him and his own well honed nostrils. In the event of it becoming a face bending, nose grabber of a lethal keeler, he then knew of nothing better than to get his feet in his shoes on a quick running route for the door. He stood where he was, as he sucked in his breath and held it there down as far into his lungs as it would go, while he thought about what he could do next. Eventually, he decided to close both of his eyes. When he slowly began to realise that he could not seem to smell whatever it was he imagined he had as much as he could before, he opened one of his eyes, though, for the moment, not the other, noticing with a heap of surprise as he did so how cramped in small his supposed new home looked and indeed was. It struck him in the brain as a probable thing that much of the space of which there was such an evident lack, had been taken out of the original hall building plan in a deliberate act of encouragement for each occupant of the apartment, with the intention of shaping the various, the peculiar and the obviously strangely formed, to fit tight in a certain, acceptable mould. One which sat well in the fatted heads of those who were known to be of a not necessarily accepting persuasion. With one eye open and one eye closed, Woller still stood and tried to find a way of only half looking to see whatever might be closest to him. This appeared to be the door of which there was only one. Without moving his feet, at first he reached out only a hand to touch the surface. And then, to bang on it with a knuckled fist. The door felt and sounded slight enough to be made of a thin sheet of wood. Then he swivelled his feet, reached out with his other hand and knocked it against the wall on his left. This time, the sound of his knocking came back at him in hollowed tones and he realised that what looked like a wall was less than much of a one, being more of a thinner divide even than the door partition that wobbled when he knuckled it. He supposed that if a smell wanted to leak, coming sneaking through and in, then, whatever thin walled space he had to call his own was a place to be sneaked in on. All of which caused him to let out a quiet noo wah through his teeth, knowing as he did that this would not be a good thing. Hauling his mind back to the point of the moment, he stretched both of his arms up to the ceiling which he found he could not reach no matter how high on his toes he pushed himself off the floor. Still in his standing spot, he shouted out in annoyance before kicking a shoe, quick at a leg of the bed which was hard and without give apart from the whack it sent, in a flash through his foot, sending him up as it did so with a lurching hop as he tried to grab a hold with both hands at wherever the hurting was coming from. Losing his balance as a result, Woller fell on his back with a thump, hard on the floor. He lay there for a moment without moving even the smallest of his bones so that if one or more of them had taken a cracking whack, nothing would crack wider than he wanted it to do. Some things seemed as they ever had, he thought. But then he was caught with the realisation that if it were not for his new got, vague, though, nonetheless, elevated status as a researcher, he would not even have been offered the use of a door shut place of his own. And he knew that this would have been an even lower done thing. Still, it remained in his head that this new, cramped in small for the moment home, was way down on the list when compared to the various places he had lived in, earlier than then. Consequently, he reckoned that being way down listed for whatever the reason was not a thing on which a finker ought to be keen. It was evident that the given accommodation in which he was then standing was well pushed in tight for room, though it was noticeable that even in such a small space, the part of the floor at which he was then looking was on a higher level than the part of the floor at the other end of the apartment from where he was – the downward or the upward slope, depending on the direction he was facing, being at least three inches up or down at its highest or at its lowest point. He was minded to think of this as nothing more than a shoe trod quirk. Then, he was pleased to discover that on walking to the top of the three inch rise to be stood at the high end of the wall in the none too big window, he could see out of it just enough to know that it looked out in the direction of, though, strangely, not quite over, the river Welland. It occurred to him that he could reach up a hand to open this window in the hope of letting go whatever keeling fumes had come in to slow melt his own brain. And so he did, opening the window as wide as it would go while heaving down and in a breather of the freshening air. Feeling better, he leaned back inside but as he did so he became aware of something which seemed to compound the sense of disappointment brought on by the somewhat harsh and less than wanted arrangements. This something was that the apartment which had been allocated to him had the appearance of being already occupied with an evident scattering of the matter of someone else everywhere to be seen. Hum ha, thought Woller to himself, as he sat down on the floor to wait for a heel kicking, long length of time before an eventual sound of boots at the top of the stairs came to a stop on the other side of the door from where he was. When the handle turned and the door was opened from the outside, a boot wearer, *the* boot wearer in question, the scatterer of matter which was still there, appeared with a mumbled apology for the late moving of both his own self and his belongings. He then began to collect whatever he had earlier scattered about, from wherever it was he had done so. As Woller looked on, the collector of matter held out a hand and introduced himself as the later than ought to have been gone researcher, otherwise known by his actual name which he said was Oscar Sollermon. With no hint of a warning he then began to talk in a sudden come rush of sounded meaning, only some of which could Woller understand until his ears caught the speeding gist about being born on a bright morning in April on the inside of a smaller than it could have been, fallen in house on the edge of the Wash, overlooking the salt flats across from the Toft jetty. And because of this low down turning out into the stark air of the fen lands, there were no expectations of becoming much more than poorly off gone without a hoped for slice of even a caking of grime. Consequently, Oscar Sollermon said to Woller he had spent too long before then whacking his fists against his own head in an attempt to crack open the disappointments and the frustrations which had shouldered him lower than he thought it was possible even for a man like him, to go. It was, however, he continued, in easier spoken words, sooner and not later when he was struck with the realisation that there was a way for him to go higher than lower on down which was to boot his feet for a searching run over the fen to take the entrance exam for the civilian service. At that time, this was beginning to operate throughout the district and was charmingly housed, as he then reckoned, in Thorney Abbey. As he listened to Oscar Sollermon loosing off his talking words, Woller tried to remember a conversation he once had with a particular someone about whom he could recall not much at all, other than that she had spoken to him about how the entrance into a service of whatever kind was a usual thing to be done at that time, regardless of subsequent finking opinion. The wrong thing to be thought was sometimes the right thing waiting to be bought, she had said. And so Oscar Sollermon had wandered his own way right on through to a quick won place amongst the lower ranks of the local administration. But then, the predicted, the predictable and the brain cracking inevitable that would have been his from the opening note of the whistle blown go was suddenly and without even a hinted warning, swept clean away with news of the unusual events at Pode Hole. In his worded telling of this to Woller, he claimed that if he had known more than he thought he then knew about the imaginings of what it would be to do and how it would have been to be done, he would have taken a steering clear to leave his own self behind and out of sight. However, for the without thinking without wanting action of him being involved, Oscar Sollermon was talking told by his friends and those who knew him that he had acquitted himself well in what been seen as the whack cracking middle of the matter. The only words he was known to have spoken about this were of the surprise in his own mind to find that even though he had been almost drawn in his brain with exhaustion at the time, having been where he was for the entire duration, he was reckoned by a late examining medicine man to have suffered only a minor state of confusion which had been sustained at a climactic moment. It seemed to be an obvious enough thing to the listening Woller that the unusual events at Pode Hole had etched a significant line of experience on Oscar Sollermons mind. In a manner common, however, to those who were listed as being there at the time, he was either reluctant to speak much more about it than he spoke or he could simply not find the speaking words to loose off the sounds he needed to make. When he did say more than a few words in the immediate, following weeks of being there, he said only that he had been offered a less than more choice opportunity of sorts.

It was a fervent hope that for those who were encouraged to attend the convalescent clinic at Gedney Hill mill, each of them would have seen the confusion which had been sustained during the unusual events at Pode Hole eased to a better form. With the eventual aim being to restore their confused minds to clear thinking. At least, it *was* a fervent hope in the minds of the founders of the clinic, earlier on, closer then to the beginning. In practice, however, those confused individuals who were there to be given ease from the confusing thoughts had experienced no easing of their confusion in any way. As a result of this, the very notion of convalescing was soon enough a source of confusion which was a stranger turn than could have been imagined by the founders of the clinic. Worse than this, it seemed to be the case that those who were keener than most on the continuing use of the clinic for the treatment of such confusion, were the same sort who were responsible for encouraging the unusual events at Pode Hole in the first place. Although, even without a point being argued, the confusion in the minds of each and all the convalescents was sudden, quick, cured in a flash which was a more peculiar occurance than ever before. Stranger still, it was understood much less than would have been thought by those who were supposed to know how such a clearing cure could indeed come about. And then with no hint of a warning, each and all of them were gone, as a clinic of former convalescents vanished without a trace. There were some who were not so concerned about these vanishing convalescents. And there were others who could only wonder about *where* they might have gone, either as one and all or each going out on their own. As a consequence of this, there were also some who assumed that the short term experiment for the correction of confusion would be forgotten, though, there were others again who understood that it would long be remembered for all the wrong reasons.

Oscar Sollermon was struck to the core with annoyance at the various recommendations that had started to be issued with a soon come regularity, more than a few of which were the least wanted and the least inviting on further close inspection. In spite of this, he allowed his own feelings no room to influence his continued broad smiling. On recognising his resulting and embarrassed need to do what could be done, even though he knew that what could be done was less than only just enough, he settled his mind at the end of a long thought on a dedicated pursuit of something which he reckoned he would call the studied meaning of finking reason. It had been at this point, he said, to Woller, when he saw that his reckoning needed some more thinking. Aware that he was a keener for some mending of the more than several flaws in his dedication, he stopped with his deciding and started instead on a head scratched, chin rubbed solution to the problem which proved to be easier in the thinking than in the doing. It was, however, sooner and not later that Oscar Sollermon sat down on a chair and pulled both it and his own self close up to a desk on which he then placed the means for scrawling down his coming words. In a remarkable show of leaping faith, his first worded go had been published by Silvester Guillory in a not much remembered collection of essayed scrawls by other wonderers too on the how and the why and the what to do about matter, if doing was the thing to be done. Even so, it had been a beginning. Somewhere to ease his lingering sense of confusion. Woller continued to listen as Oscar Sollermon then talking told him how, at the time of his first knocking a hand on the door of the cramped in small apartment, he had become either well known or easily knowable as both a scrawler of some promise and a critical finker too. Which one, he could not be sure. On the question of a knock, he explained that Woller had made a quicker than expected appearance a while before he had gotten around to picking up his boots and his shirts and his hangers for the lugged heaving of his moveable means which he then began to move as he spoke. That which could be moved and gone, was. And in spite of his being ceased as he was from the work of a researcher at the School of Thought, attached to Ayscoughfee Hall, he had secured a low scrawling position on an enquiring journal so that all he needed then was a roof under which he could place a chair for the sitting in or on, whenever he had the time to do so. After a heave ho-ing of me, no me, yes me, not you, negotiation on a price for a cash handing over with a vendor of less than little shift but more than much of a definite shiftiness, Oscar Sollermon eventually succeeded in getting his long itching fingers on the keys to three rooms of his own calling in a large red brick house which sat high on the bank looking out over the open fields of Cowbit Wash. Then as sharp as he had begun, he came to a sudden quick end of his own telling, saying only that it was as smack on the mattering nose as it ought to be, suggesting instead that the two of them each and the other foot, boot and leg it off to the boozer for a thirst stopping bottle of hand clutched booze. Woller reckoned this was a better way of heel kicking than most and was through the door, then down the stairs in a long gone flash, leaving the former researcher trailing in his wake.

Oscar Sollermon, sooner and not later, after this collided
meeting, became a first called listener for Woller on the other
end of a telephone line. And as a consequence, one of his
closest known friends who was ever present if needed to be. A
keener of a talker, a happening now doer and a shovelling in
guzzler, as well as being a refiner of a diner and a without cause
to be asked imbiber, he was also a slick handed briber, though
always a charmer and an entertaining finker on his own two
comical feet. Well knowing about certain corrupted notions,
he also realised that there were some who thought of him as no
good for his own self and who considered it a necessary thing
to make an observing note of what they saw as his swerving
behaviour and his actual, used words, whether scrawled down
or spoken out loud. There were others who were thought to
be annoyed at his presence, loose holding on, as each and all
of them were to a slackening of taste with their own gossiping
chatter and accusations of bought and fancied pretence. What
could be known only to him would be used to ensure the
better condition of his own mattering means, knowing well,
more than most, how to use the chattering of the fennermarsh
people and the various finking members of both the Gosberton
Clough and the Tydd Gote cultural elites to his own advantage.
With considerable ease, he had learned how to become a
valuable man to be known, keeping out of close chattered reach
of those who were keen to hide their own soiled hands and who
were therefore quieter than they might otherwise have been.
On the question of his finking work, he was considered, by his
friends and those who knew him, to be a better teller of well
wrought tales in his own scrawled down words than he was at
telling them in the actual talking words as they were talked by
almost everyone else scattered throughout the wider fen lands.
The prolific author of seven, earlier celebrated, disquisitions
of scrawler fink which were reckoned by just about all of

those finkers who read them to be straight on the lean of the meaning as it was meant, he was the closest thing to an equal, both in sensibility and finking creativity, whom Woller had yet met. Although, it was possible that none of these things could have predicted the immediate ease that was struck with such familiarity against their each held differences in temperament even if this might have been supposed to be a gone wheeling cog, spun off on its own. In the case of the one, Oscar Sollermon was a whirring, purring, flamgadding bonner and a no doubt about it, suited banger of elegant noise, whereas, in the case of the other, Woller could be, if he would be and he *would* be, if he were *obliged* to be but without much of the *wanting* to be what was wanted of him or whatever was thought of him by those people who did not know him. Only some of which was what he thought of his own self. Instead, for Woller, it was about finking and less than much else. Oscar Sollermon was minded to think of this as being cracked in the head strange, taking no account, as he would, of a need to pull out the mattering means of each day and establish in his brain that his circumstances were as he had left them or had changed their shape, no more than they often did, as time bong handed its way past his line of sight. If there was something about which he might have been more than otherwise concerned, it was the assured brand of radical posturing that had become, in his own mind at least, a deep held and serious matter, even though he took only a glancing notice of his friends and those who knew him when they warned him about such heard right opinions as could draw what attention of his could be drawn, to a potential heaping of derision on his finking reputation. Their earlier, anxious, clearing of throats, had been caught sharp and frit at Oscar Sollermons come out of nowhere association with several anarchic tendencies. And his probable dependence on them and their berserker associates, if he were to be cut off from his other more usual contacts. However, he had for a long time gone been a recognised seeker of change and in various ways he sometimes tried to convert Woller to the same need for the same ideal, by way of showing him that his aptitude *for* and his attitude *to* the mattering means was, in essence, not a different one to that of the anarchist tendency or of the other factions that shared similar values with the anarchic committees, collectives and collectivists all. But Oscar Sollermon was well enough clear about the ease at which others could be fritted up scared and legged off quick, screaming out loud on having their ears filled in with hurling words of berserker change. And he, therefore, made sure to keep a holding rein on that racing, fevered part of his own brain as much as he could under the circumstances. That he retained such goodwill as he did from those around him was through his knowing of people, though not in a way which allowed him to claim to know what was on the inside of the minds of some — just that he knew and he was known by more people than most other people could ever want to do or to be. There were those who thought of him as a quiet to use smoother for a polite shake of a meeting or for a fleeting, careering push at a giver of sweetening juice. And others still who needed his touch for a fumbled greeting of cheating fingers and flickering tongues in a cornered off somewhere, with another someone in the dark. But of all the people who were known to Oscar Sollermon, there was one individual in particular who was of a bigger way set than the rest of them all put together in a finking heap and this was Thelonius Greeling. And of all those people who looked on Oscar Sollermon as a friend, there was indeed one finker in need who had a queue jumpingly keen interest in Thelonius Greeling. This finker was Woller, who had not yet forgotten Oscar Sollermons earlier worded mention that the personal connection of importance which he had used to land himself an offer from the scrawlers at an enquiring journal, was, indeed, made real in the person of Thelonius Greeling. Consequently, the thinking of a question for Woller was a simple enough thing. Would he be curious to meet Thelonius Greeling? For someone with a marker as sharp as his could be, Oscar Sollermon was more than less aware of just how much of a keening there was on the inside of Wollers mind. And he knew too that it was not the sort of question to which a starting out finker with fewer than not significant, personal contacts of his own making would ever consider turning down. It, therefore, caused him no big surprise when Woller said that he would.

Although Thelonius Greeling had only gone with his own self
to the fields and the running creeks which lay flattened out in
all directions from the edges of Wisbech, on the rarest of
occasions, in, what then seemed to him, to be an ever
lengthening period of time, his reputation throughout the
wider fen lands was of a bigger than otherwise standing to have
been knocked to the back of a finkers mind or allowed him to
be forgotten. As a result, his name was as celebrated then
among those of a not often finking sort as well as those for
whom the meaning of a finking being was all there might be.
As it had always been. His own scrawler fink work was a
constant source of scandalised wonder and the state of his
careering progress was in no small way the chatter squawked
cause of much more than all different kinds of earnest
speculation, confused asking and a hoped for reckoning with a
scratching of heads. And the confusion was further slipped
down with his friends and those who knew him, his far from
friends and even those who had really no catching hold of what
it was that he did or how it was done. On the inside of his own
bones, Thelonius Greeling was whacked out and knackered
with the thinking about, the understanding of and the
accepting of whoever he might or might not be or whoever he
may or may not have been before, a long time earlier than then.
He tried not to think about who he could become, later than
now, as he was not so much keen and less than more convinced
in his own mind of the value of a given out, handed down
stamper of identification, a recognition or an etched marking in
a bright coloured ink. This seemed to Woller to be a twisting of
collected matter that rang close to the jib of his own brained
curious skidding through the thinking of thoughts, the
scrawling of words and the staring out at the fen lands that only
at its easiest might become snagged for long enough to be seen
clean. Such a caring lack for the pindownability of things was

the cause for an equal removal of approval amongst certain
people, in certain quarters, in which the right thing was never
the wrong thing, though it could and it would have been more
than much in the wringing of concerned hands, had it been
made known to them just what other finking matters Thelonius
Greeling had been doing, somewhere that was elsewhere.
Without either the seeing or the hearing of those of a
censorious sort. With a noted difference to the manner of some
of those with whom Woller had shaken hands during his recent
times, people who had talked louder about both promise and
their own promises than the keeping of either, Oscar Sollermon
was as good as his word. It occurred to him that he could be so,
as he sometimes was, because of the assured sense of belonging
he had found on the inside of a group of hang around finkers
who were more often than otherwise to be found in the
company of Thelonius Greeling, who, in his own way, regarded
Oscar Sollermon with a smiling affection which flickered quick
at the corners of his mouth. Each of those who were there, to
be strung out and hung long with a personal wanting of finking
words, to scrawl down his ideas and to cut off the slack for
themselves on favourable terms, were well knowing that
Thelonius Greeling was an encouraging voice for curious, new
come finkers. A keener for those who might be of possible
interest to his own mind, provided they were, in turn and in
order to be included, minded to fit themselves around the
required numbering details of his usual supper time plans. In
spite of his reckoning of whatever it might be that was
necessary for the appropriate numbers to be understood, being
less even than nought though bigger than a single one in a space
of its own, it was a queasily brain stopping calculation which
pushed him to be sat down on a chair for fear of falling off with
a balancing loss. Thelonius Greeling, nonetheless, agreed to
Oscar Sollermons request for Woller to be invited to the

whenever next supper time occasion he was hoping to host.
There was, however, a complication on the day in question
when it seemed that in addition to those numbered chairs at the
table which were used to seat the members of the family
Greeling, there were to be more than expected numbers of
sitters, on more of the seats than could be numerically allowed.
The late inclusion of one more would then wallop on in
through the whole, forcing open the cracks in Thelonius
Greelings peculiar mind. In a fortunate happening for Woller,
one of the originally invited spoon guzzlers sent their apologies
in advance of not coming which meant he was asked to go
along in their place. Although, he was then caught with
surprise when Oscar Sollermon found a moment to talking tell
him the what and the how and the when and the what not. And
also the how not and the when not of the words to be used
when he was there. Oscar Sollermon did not explain his
reasons and Woller did not ask. When the time of the supper
time dine came around, on the supping down night as it was,
Woller pitched himself up at the white painted front door of the
red brick town house on the river Nene, in which Thelonius
Greeling lived with the other members of his family and a dog.
And pushing forward a finger, he rang the bell. The noise it
made was not a ring but a shortening ding which Woller
thought was a har de har of a thing that made him press it again
as he stood where he was, feeling awkward and ill fitted in the
formal clothes he had chosen to wear. Then, sooner than he
had time to pull at the sleeves of his jacket or run a finger
around the collar of his shirt, the door was opened from the
inside by Cordelia Greeling who ushered him through to the
dining room. Sitting on a chair at the table, he was still feeling
not quite of the correct shape fitting when he was caught with
the sudden realisation that the food had all been eaten,
appearing as it did that supper time was properly done and

gone, even though the other members of the family had not been at the table to eat with the invited shovellers. And aside from Cordelia Greeling, he had neither seen them or heard their voices coming from anywhere else in the house. It took him a moment to decide how much of a hum ha strange thing he might be minded to think all this was. Stranger than otherwise, he eventually thought. There was one snuffler on which he had laid a cornering eye and that was the dog or what could be seen of the dog, as there was not much he could see other than its occasionally wagged, long black tail, protruding out from under the chair on which Thelonius Greeling was sat. He assumed there was more dog to it than that out of sight of his own looking, not least because of the wagging bit of it that *could* be seen. And which when it was not in motion, remained laid out flat. Just as he was wondering whether he might get down on to the carpeted floor to take a closer look, sudden time and quick, Thelonius Greeling stood up from his chair without speaking a word and strode away from the table. Accordingly, Woller also rose to follow as each of the other clean shovelled guzzlers got up and followed the striding Thelonius Greeling as he went through to another room, in which there was an open fire burning in the grate and a worn gathering of well cushioned armchairs pulled up close in a loop around it. Thelonius Greeling sat his bones down in a flop, deep in what appeared to be his own favourite armchair which it was obvious enough at a glance, could be seen to be a better shaped, more comfortable and an altogether fatter one than the other chairs placed about it. Almost all of those who were there for such a shortened time continued to stand on their feet, either stood low on their soles in leather tight shoes or balanced high on their heels in delicate straps, as glasses of hand clutched booze were then drunk, down and in as the spooners became boozers who boozed and talked out loud more than each of them had before. Thelonius

Greeling made a less than most effort to speak, looking more concerned, as he did, only to be sat, apparently smiling, just to be listening to the word chattered sounds that filled the air close by his ears with the talking small and the talking big, the chattering sounds and the spoken words which sounded like things that needed to be said. Woller stood where he could. Which meant he was standing to one side of those who were gathered around the open fire, each of them talking words without listening too hard to the sounds that were made. From deep in his cushioned slump, Thelonius Greeling looked over at Woller who he could see was standing with his own self without much speaking to anyone else. And as he did so, Woller looked across at Thelonius Greeling, sitting with his own self and not much speaking either, seemingly still and no less content to listen to the raised, the lowered, the rounded and the slurred, the wobbled and the drawled, rhythms of the chatterers about him. And sometimes peering, with a hint of a squint, at whatever he could mostly see through the thick lenses of his ebony rimmed spectacles. Such a glancing exchange, seemed to Woller, to be one of those curious moments of meaning without speaking which came easy enough through a well known respect between two minded finkers, each and the other. And better again, he knew that if his own finking mind had been acknowledged by Thelonius Greeling then he would be with no weighted lack, recognised wherever he went, throughout and about the wider fen lands of the east and the west and the north and the south. And though he was less than more sure of the recognising matter, he thought this could be a good thing. Even so, he was more than aware of being at a big time loss on understanding exactly what it was that a friend was or was not, so that a new met acquaintance who might be or might not, seemed to be as confusing a thing to be thought much about. Instead of which he tried his own mind at thinking on the lines of other thoughts. And without knowing why, he thought about the rest of the dog and how it would look when seen with more than a tail, black on the carpet and under a chair. When he then found this harder to understand than the question of the how or the what or who was a friend and who was not, he became a sudden keener to clear off with his own means for a while of some laid down rest. And so he did, saying his goodbyes to Thelonius Greeling and the hung about boozers as he shoe, legged it off, away from the noise.

The learning work that Woller was expected to do, as a researcher, at the School of Thought, attached to Ayscoughfee Hall, could not have been thought of as particularly demanding by anyone, under any circumstances but he quick time realised that he was fortunate in the extreme as there appeared to be only a single new come student who was in need of his attention. The curious individual in question was a young woman who had not long before arrived at the school from Terrington St. Clement in the eastern fen and who was clever minded enough to be as fleet as she could with the sort of intelligence which would put her straight down on the same talking and the same finking keel as Woller himself. She was a charmer of a talker and a woozer of a looker who drew both long and short looks from those who happened to be there, wherever it was she might have been. On the matter of learning and being learned, she was reckoned on knowing as much of the given out means as she had been allowed at the school. As a consequence, she was keening sharp on filling herself up to the brimming top with more and not less of the otherwise thought and the odder wrought words and ideas as she could be told or at least whatever it was Woller could tell her. A first time go for some talking to and looking through the worded pages of those finkers, scrawlers and quoters who were well enough thought, had earlier been agreed, when each of them spoke to the other on the telephone to arrange a starting hour of eleven o clock in the morning on the following day. And it was, therefore, at this exact moment that she came to be stood on the outside of the door to the cramped in small apartment, wondering if it was the one she was looking for. After a short while, she was minded to think of him either being there or not, so she started a loud rapping with her knuckles on the flimsy wood of the door which buckled under the force of the blows without taking less than much effect as to the thing being opened. She decided that rather than stand waiting for however long it might take, she ought to open it herself and go through to the inside. And so she did. The cramped in small apartment was cramped in small enough for the bed to be close up to where she was surprised to be sudden time standing and looking at what appeared to be, stretched out on its length, a snooze grunting, tall shape of a man who was not only doing nothing but sleeping, he was making even less than much of any sort of movement other than none. She reckoned on being in not such a rush as to need to wake the flat gone Woller from his grunt snoozelling sleep and after some hesitation, she scrawled down a brief note of worded explanation about her arriving, her looking and her waited, head scratch wondering about what she might do, before putting it next to his head as she left. When, eventually, he had come round from sleeping and was awake enough to read her note, Woller was caught in the throat at the suggestion that they meet at a later time on the same day in a spoongrease dinner shop, there in the town. On his first imagining of the possible harm he could come to from the keeling smells and the residue of grease, Woller decided that in no way could he turn himself up at the suggested place and be expected to stay for longer than a single heave of his lungs. But he did not want to seem to be a worried barker, as someone for other people to worry themselves about and so he went along all the same, attempting to think himself pleased to be going somewhere on what had become a bright, snap tearing day, with the wind flattening out through the streets and taking breath without warning, in a shock and a sudden thudding in to chill, rattled bones. Outside, it was fen stark and cold and in no small way because of the absence of warmth to be found in the open, there was a crowding mass of huddlers seated on cheap plastic benches, on the inside of the spoongrease dinner shop, the air itself thickened with steam and the slow rising warmth of those guzzlers who were there, moving as they did, in a quickening flash of shovelling hands and of handled forks. The grease from the kitchen was hauled down and in, then followed through with a scalding slurp from the brimming, clinking mugs which were clutched in hands, each and all. As he walked through the slurping, shovelling crowd, on turning himself up, through and in the door, with his breathing held down and his nostrils snuffled in tight, Woller could see that all the tables were crammed with guzzlers spooning in grease, except for one at which was sat, alone on a chair, a someone who he was minded to think of as an obvious enough case for being his expectant meeter. After a few goes at breathing while making his way across the room, it seemed to be easier than he thought and he was close on considering his bones as being sat down without quick running out and gasping a breather in the door opened air. To breathe without concentrating on the how of his doing so at all had become less than more of a concern which he thought of as a good thing. And so, with a better feeling of where he was stood, he reached out a hand to be shook and introduced himself to his new and indeed, his only student. There was a pulling of smiles and a small talking moment before the two of them, each and the other, decided, with an awkward cough and a buttoned tug, to work out a way of doing what it was that needed to be done, so that she could be given the learning which she certainly wanted. Woller then confessed that in spite of his supposed expertise as a researcher, he had not really, had not ever, sort of known how to make someone other than him become learned or to talking tell them how to learn for themselves. This was quite different again and much more than less difficult to do. He rubbed one hand on his chin, hum ha how. And he scratched his head with the other, ha hum why but he came up with nothing of use apart from a vague, shoulder heaved motion as he sat, alone, on the inside of his own wondering mind. It then occurred to him with a sudden quick thought that what was much needed was something more than a suggested list of recommended words. What was needed more than before was a spark to the brain, a quickening lick with a following kick of its own triggered means. And so he decided on a telling out loud account of a long gone fennerman of finking note who had been much earlier known.

Counsellor Milton was who he was and could never have
been anyone else, someone without the freedom to choose or
to decide for his own self, the whatever and the whoever, the
however and the whenever of being or not. At no time had
he allowed himself to become pinned down with a particular
sort of dog eared barking but then neither had he excluded his
own self or opposed any one point of view. And even if he was
less than much keen on the wagging of a mardy old tale and a
barker of slogans of the right and the wrong, he was completely
in favour of the right of the teller to be a shouter or a hurler of
words or maybe he *was* long before, earlier than then. There
were times when it seemed harder to remember and easier to
forget, though he was never a flincher from wanting to know,
being able and eager to see things from a wherever gone view.
When it came to his own voice talking or the telling of a tall
enough tale, these were the better heard words of whichever
gathered place he was in − without for a beat, making a self
fancied sort, giving way as he would to anyone else who had
something to be said. Counsellor Milton was, therefore, a well
sought comer to come through a door. A hipper, a ripper and
a tipper of delight, a fizzer of a figure to have at the centre of a
crowd, haw hawing a haw with whom so ever was there to be
hard talked and haw hawed with. All there was, was there to
be seen, as lean and as clean as it could be. In spite of having
no right and no wrong of his own, he was reckoned to be a
profoundly moral and compassionate man, seeing cynicism as a
stopper to be overcome, to be cracked on down with a smooth
order of oomph until it was out and out gone. The oomph
which he wanted was a cracker of the bright and the new. He
was curiouser than most and was thought of as being so, not
least for the chew of the meaning to be known. And because
he had squeezed his own mattering means skim to the brim
with a sense of release, it occurred to him that he might then be

a squeezing releaser for other wheezers too, close as he was to
a working method which could be used to pin down a notion
of how a thing looked as it did, from both the outside and the
inside, either from above or below. He was held with a need to
understand the when of his own time, in which it was easier to
be brought low with a thump than it was to find comfort for the
bones and the brain. What he wanted was wonder, the keening
of the senses, how to see, how to think, how to be, how to learn,
how to know. And how to do it all with a well observed guffaw
and a low down honk. To cut a hack in the wear and a rent in
the weave of muddling gonzers everywhere, for not doing what
could be done. Woller came to a stop with his talking words
and looked at the girl from Terrington St. Clement. It was an
easy enough thing to be seen that his sudden quick telling had
served them both well as a settler of personal nerves, to the
point where nothing seemed to be worse than it usually did, at
other times and with different people. In a same like manner,
Woller and the girl from Terrington St. Clement, the pair of
them together, continued on in the same learning manner on
the following afternoons at the spoongrease dinner shop until
all that could be learned or heard about Counsellor Milton,
Professor Quiller, the moodlers, the boomers and the clatterers
too, was caught fast in her brain for the staying. The concern
for Woller was that the talking and the listening was more than
much of whatever he could have imagined it to be, knowing as
he did that somewhere deep, down and in, his fascination sat in
a different place to the one he had expected. This was not one
of a thinking lean but a feeling that came as a less than familiar
reeling, throwing him sharp out of kilter, as it seemed he had
taken a curious fancy to the young woman with her finking
mind and the shape of her smile. This caused him to think, as
he did, about how he was as confused by the speed of his own
response as much as the why and the when of whatever course

of action he could take, with a someone he could take it with or not. All of which made him feel queasy enough to lie down on a vacant floor and close his eyes against the madness.

One of the matters of soon coming importance, in the mind of Thelonius Greeling, at least, according to some, was that the first week of the month would see the appearance of the boomercumlingo document in an enquiring journal. And as such, it occurred to Woller that he might push his own, earlier asked for contribution with quieted ease into the hurl of words that had sudden time been loosed off by his friends and those who knew him. There was a wondering in his brain as to why he was more than usually bone gone rattled by the distraction of the girl from Terrington St. Clement than by the destruction of the thing, it had been decided, was under almost immediate threat. Although he was less than more sure about this, it could be seen only in the light of his feeling freeze which was how he thought he ought to see it. And so he did. It was then later than sooner that he wondered if it might be a good thing if he were never to remind himself of how the girl from Terrington St. Clement had come to be a welling giver of bewildering, fink boggling misery for him of a sort that he had not known before. When, only a short time earlier, she had been a smiler of contentment just to sit with him close, for a lengthened talk about Counsellor Milton, Professor Quiller, the moodlers, the boomers and the clatterers too. Worse was to come in just the second week of the month when she loose skirt hitched and cloddered off with a smaller and lesser looking man than him, from somewhere on the edge of Gedney Dyke. The girl from Terrington St. Clement did not tell Woller why she had done this, only that she had. And Woller did not ask. He only knew he was sad that she had. This was something he thought of as a bad thing and as a rum thing, as a ha thing and as a hum thing. Ha hum. And it then became even more of a no good thing when both the girl from Terrington St. Clement and her new found, following man, attended together, each and the other, a meeting of assorted finkers, in the silver painted tin hut, of the members of the Tydd Gote collective, at which Woller sat on a chair at the back, alone with his own self. The meeting had been called on account of the rumoured, soon come appearance of the boomercumlingo document in an enquiring journal. And its proceedings were pulled to order by a stern talking Silvester Guillory who made what he could of an attempt to marshal the surprise forcing together of the various opinions and argued certainties of some of those who were present. It seemed that most of those, though, not all, were intent on throwing out of the only window to be found a chance of a harmonious exchange of quietly done talking rather than one of loud, shouted words. Although, because Thelonius Greeling himself was seen to there, the louder shouters held themselves in check from their threatened annoyance at the recent thoughts of those who more than otherwise annoyed them. And as result of such restraint, the meeting stayed hung to a balance without falling in on the finkers who were there. But even caught as he was in the hurling noise around him, it seemed to Woller, sat on a chair in his own loose knocking bones, as though there was almost no sound to be heard on the outside of his head. And nowhere else to look other than down at the floor, around his own two shoed feet or at the girl from Terrington St. Clement and her man from somewhere on the edge of Gedney Dyke. And what was then already less than good took a sudden quick lurch over to the worse than bad as together, both at the same time, in the silver painted tin hut, in the presence of the members of the Tydd Gote Collective, the girl from Terrington St. Clement and her Gedney Dyke man, made an announcement straight off and then of their intention to get themselves spoken for as mister and missus, the one with the other. As his hearing returned and sound again crashed in on his brain, Woller was caught in the throat and rocked back in his chair at the hair curling news. And because the moment was spurring, he leapt sharp to his feet and heel click toed his way out through the back door which he closed behind him before standing alone on the outside, in the dark, in the rain, again.

Those editorial scrawlers who made the decisions that made the matter of publication happen, were aware that Thelonius Greeling and his elaborately obscure, though, nonetheless, popular work could be a saving and graceful means of not running on cash emptied accounts. And so without a leaping of surprise to those grafters who did not make the choices but who made all the effort, a decision was come to that each of them would begin to serialise the whatever and the however shortened word pieces which were to be commissioned from Thelonius Greeling at the earliest possible time. What was not seen in advance, either by them or by him, was the problem of the sudden found annoyance of his ebony rimmed spectacles which were now giving him serious trouble. Having so far undergone nine operations and four technical alterations in order to find some kind of a solution to the wearing aggravation, it was a matter of concern that nothing to have been tried by those of the specialising kind, had appeared to be close to a point of success in doing this or doing that or even doing the other of what needed to be done. And then sooner and not later as had been suggested by the last to be consulted optical but a long way from far sighted expert, who had shone a light and peered after it into Thelonius Greelings right eye, then his left eye and then his right eye again, there was a catastrophic happening and he lost the means of seeing anything at all through the lenses of his ebony rimmed spectacles. It was so bad that he could not even read his own scrawled words. As a consequence of this, he was grumpingly obliged to visit, several times each week, the specialist who claimed for himself an expertise in the mending of ebony rimmed spectacles at a clinic in Quadring Eaudyke which was not just the place to go, it was also the only way in which a solution could be found to resolve the issue which had now whacked him hard with a fumbling squint. Thelonius Greelings sense of his own isolation was sooner and not later more than he could tolerate, sending him off quick time and sudden to what he reckoned was the obvious enough conclusion of finding a way of seeing for himself. So he cushioned his bones down in his favourite armchair and began to think about just what to do. After a long while of thinking and wondering, he gave his head an eventual scratch. Then he pulled on his ears and snorted through his nostrils until, eventually, he settled his mind on the possibilities of super magnification with the aid of two large magnifying glasses, each one taped over of each of his eyes which would allow him to read on almost as he had done before. When the contraption was rigged together, however, by his own two bodging hands, he discovered that it would not begin to be effective unless he was more than less reclined in a back leaning chair. Otherwise, the weight of the pretending to be lenses caused them to move out of position or to fall straight off his face as he tried to look through at what he could see of his immediate surroundings which made it hard for him to even consider being sat at his desk to start work on editing the shortened word pieces which were still raw in his own handed scrawl. So he asked Woller to help. At the sound of this, on his end of a telephone line, Woller was knocked clear to the side and bashed on the ear at the asking of such a question from such a finker at such a time. Although he was not even at the end of the beginning as a scrawler himself without much of a mention as to his own bare knowing about how he might be of assistance, he said yes, he would do what he could to make sure all the pages were filled with the appropriate words. Thelonius Greeling announced that he was happier than before to have asked Woller to help out with the matter in question and said all that remained was for Woller to pitch himself up at the red brick town house with the white painted front door, on the river Nene, to get on with editing the words of the various shortened pieces. And so he did. When the scrawl cleaning process was complete, Woller stayed on to assist Thelonius Greeling with other scrawler fink matters such as to read out loud the words or mark the pages of a document that he thought might be of use to him and his magnified looking contraption. But he was insistent in his own talking words to his friends and those who knew him that at no time had he taken in a handed out thought. And that no brew making or scrawler smile faking was ever volunteered. Also and maybe even because he was sometimes a keener for saying the opposite to that which was, Woller agreed with those who mentioned it that both he and Thelonius Greeling, each and the other, were sharers of such common held things as being new come migrants to Wisbech from the wrong parts of the fen lands with a dedication to finking. And the intriguing and the fascinating too, whether it be the high or the low or the large or the small or the gracefully tasteful or the gracelessly distasteful – even on occasion, the disgracefully graceless. It had also been noted by some of a squealing sort that the two of them were dissenting reckoners and sceptical enquirers for the sake of their autonomous minds, as each and the other were. And had to be, conscious, as each was, of keeping a reasonable finking distance from the sectarianism that had more than less often leaked its way through from the local berserkers to the cultural elites, no matter who or where they might be. Neither was either of this curious pair much in a way good at the understanding of numbers or the various calculations and combinations of patterns needed for a determined summing up by a reasonable brain. Stranger still, it seemed as though Thelonius Greeling could quicker than most become scared frit to leaping out at his own inner made superstitions, of ladders and of cats and of talking dogs and of monkeys wearing hats. In contrast, Woller was thought to have left whatever superstitious notions he had ever had buried deep under the abandoned weight of his earlier, well gone self. Smiling was good. And some things were funny, as well as peculiar too. Whereas bonkers was no more or no less than it had ever been, whether to Woller or to Thelonius Greeling, either of whom was a goner for a laugh with few bars to a hold. However, of the how for or the when for or the what for or even the why for, of that which was considered to be uniting, none of it was made an obvious thing by Thelonius Greeling through the words he spoke to anyone or no one else. It would, he said, be a less than usual sound for him to make, to holler out loud about having discovered a startling new talent with a promising future as a finker amongst the best of the finking establishment there was to be found. And so he made not a worded sound on the matter. There were some who had noted in their gathering files that what he *could* have done was of less than much interest to him, with the argument being that for each clutcher gorged self there were such things as the ranking of a name in the minds of those who might care. Who some imagined *would care about* or *despair of* the way up heights or the low down depths of a reputation in question. What *was* gone from the brain of Thelonius Greeling was a need to consider the wants of those other careering finkers who might end up better at the doing of it than him which meant that his generosity had a lesser reach than its potential. But no matter what could be thought of him, by some, Thelonius Greeling was more than otherwise known to be a leaper for joining a crowd of thirsters in a heaving, goofer stained boozer, to drink, swift down and in, the swilling booze. While he was stood at the bar, clamping a hand on a glass and beaming out a smiler to the company he was keeping, he would be well reckoned on it being a necessary lean for his own fragile self, keen as it was, on a continuing stream of you are and you can and you will and we will and we do. He had barely ever been a fatted show man, even though he was fatter cut shown in a way that he thought was more than enough for his own means to be measured, for his family and for his friends and those who knew him. But for some of those who were on the outside of his brain, looking on in, at what he would consider to be an open showing, there could be less than might be thought to be seen or no more of what he seemed to think was a different shape to the one he could feel. Although, by far the oddest thing about Thelonius Greeling in the mind of Woller was that he claimed to have chucked in and given up on the question of the meedler vong without giving out an explanation as to why, not even to those who went off quick with a jab or slower with a handed clasp and a pleading kneel.

Woller had now been on the inside of the house with the red bricks, the white painted front door and the black tailed dog, almost as much as the Greeling family themselves. And because his being there was more usual than most, he had made an effort to get to know through their spoken words, the daughter to the father, who was often to be found in one room or another about the place. Sometimes she was reading a book while sat in a chair and at other times she could be seen staring out of a window at the street, as she stood without much of a twitch. Tabitha Greeling was some years younger than Woller, as well as being delicate in her bones both to look at and to touch. She had enormous green eyes and long dark hair which he noticed was more often than otherwise tied up in a loose knot at the back of her head, so that strands of it fell down her neck and over her ears. And although she seemed to be almost as nervous with him as he was with her, she had a flickering burn in her own mind that could, on occasion, be sparked into life, causing her movements to quicken and her eyes to flash bright, catching him deep in the throat and struck for a peep at their size and their colour, in the face they were in. Which reckoning as he did on wanted looks, seemed to him to be a beautiful one indeed. In spite of all this, he was not sure what he ought to do. And so he did nothing.

At the end of the month, Woller realised, in his own time, just how much of the mattering means he had crowded into being done, not least with the detailed matter of his new piece of scrawler fink which had been approved by those who selected the entered work for the critical symposium on the boomercumlingo, suggested as it had been by Thelonius Greeling himself. It had occurred to him that the suggestion had only been made as banker of flattering support but he accepted the catcher with less than he could of a blink, as there was also the possibility of scrawling down an appraisal of a way of finking as understood by Thelonius Greeling, his friends and those who knew him. And he was well knowing in his brain that this had been a point of similar wanting for a number of finkers since he had first turned himself up in Gosberton Clough when he had. So he decided to haul in the offered chance there and then. In addition to his own wrought notions, he had been lent some finking works by Oscar Sollermon who had scrawled down on each of the pages in a dark red ink, his worded opinions about the various theoretical concerns that characterised the essential meaning of the idea which he referred to as wotchermacallitosophy. When Woller said, what? Oscar Sollermon talking told him that it was not to be said or to be asked for, saying only that to do so and to ask what it was would only cause a confusion of interpretation, followed on quick with some head scratched consternation of a not wanted sort. The more it was open to being given a voice, the more it would become of interest to those who were continually on the look out for such things. And the more possibilities there were of being wrong and not right as it was understood, the more complications there would be for the individuals involved, including himself which he knew would be a bad thing. It seemed to Woller that Oscar Sollermon was making as much sense as could be made in the circumstances, even though it

would be an easier gone lurch to make, one worse than nothing
at least. And because he was less than ever before sure about
what he ought to say or what he *could* say, he said nothing at
all which might confuse the matter further. Choosing instead
a quiet approach, he scrawled down his words on the page
for the benefit of Thelonius Greeling, in recognition of the
now turning old barker and his long established methods of
working, in such circumstances as those that there were, of
the subjects to be allocated to each of the contributors. After
which he would then decide on how to explain their respective
finking merits. Woller got down to the first working version
of his piece almost before he had sat his bones flat on the chair
behind his desk, in the cramped in small apartment at the
School of Thought, attached to Ayscoughfee Hall. At the end
of a long winding think about how to proceed, he had been
kicked in the brain with the sudden realisation that he would
need to research the subject which for a researcher such as he
was ought not be such a difficult thing for him to do. In the
notes he had made for Woller to read, Oscar Sollermon had
asserted that the boomercumlingo had been adapted from an
earlier work on a similar theme but with the words taken out
and then changed and arranged for a different reading with a
new way of meaning before being put back on the page again,
in a less than usual order. Also, in his well noted humming and
his best quoted harring, he appeared to suggest that the whole
of it was an attempt by Thelonius Greeling to understand the
cog worn marking of his own mind which he thought was a
good enough angle for Woller to run, clean and lacking a tweak.
Woller, however, was less than pleased to accept a down handed
opinion from anyone, not least one that gave a barely complete
explanation of the author's thoughts about a cause for all the
trouble he saw. And although he was minded to think of this
as something he could well do without he was curious enough

about Oscar Sollermons well meaning notes to read through them again, starting with a clattering attempt on Gauntlet Bridge by the gone stoppers of the where and when, thought to be new come from Jenkins Bank. Caught hard in need, there were means of giving them ease which none of them took until the boomer struck with a hopple and a crump, being funny peculiar more than ha ha. There were some who thought it would have suited a meedler to whistle the hooblayong while calling out over the mubbellongong, for someone who could understand a jack to a fudder. Although, with some things taken too late and some taken too soon, there was a moodle of confusion, leading others to leave with a whack of a heel, in the hang of a word, joomers jooming more and not less. Woller was struck between the ears at this, not least because there were those who seemed to be keen on a sharpening move which would lead to a crowding of open space for the finking sort. Along with the almost inevitable calls for the cracking of bones and the encouragement of dog eared barking, this could only be seen to forecast a shoe brained cropper of a fall. And so it was. Although, he was able to catch a hold of his balance again with the reading of the concluding words on the clammier than easier to tolerate happening of what it then meant to exist as a well booted, own minded individual, one who was given out with a brimming fill of having something and nothing. And having to do and not do, while stating the prerogative of a finker who might engage in a maddening cause only to scribble and scratch at the fink made self. The elegant description of a worse gone individual and the hard won flicker of whatever appeared to be done when a smile was pulled across a mouth was a source of fascination to Woller, as he started in on making his appraisal in clear worded terms. Arguing as he did that at no point could a finking mind be used in the hope of looking for recognition in what some finkers saw as an absolute, instead of the comparison of being with or being without or being nothing or something. All such points could be made at some or no particular time, according to the who and the where and the how of the making itself. With his first proper go at a nottle done scoot seen by most as a considerable success, Woller was as pleased with himself as Thelonius Greeling also seemed to be. At the same time and more than less important, so too were the assorted cacklers who were responsible for inking it out, causing Woller to be caught with a surprised relief over what he had earlier thought was a sobber of a sop to the boomercumlingo. As a consequence, however, of a common understanding about that which was implied rather than stated, with barging comparisons and scrawler fink equivalents, his work was reckoned to be the least leer cheering of all when it eventually appeared in the language of a fennermarshers publication. With a realisation that kicked in his brain, he made a handed reach for a chin rubbed think, in a head scratched moment, on the possibility of having established a theme through which he could retain sole possession over the necessity for talking and scrawling and shouting and honking out both quiet and loud sounded words. A second time, he was brain kicked again with a longing for more than ordinary experience could provide. Although what it could be, other than being more and not less than what he then had, was something on which he could not quite fasten a hold, even when it seemed obvious enough that a published appearance of his work would be bound to send his searching mind out with a leap, hurtling around from one place to another before coming to an eventual pause as a better made finker of sorts. One who could see for himself the heightening gap between where he had come *from* and wherever he was *going*, alone on the inside of his own mattering means.

As he had become the finker he had, it occurred to Woller, at the end of a long think that his circle of friends was beginning to widen further out than the reach of the smirking greelers and the carping punchers, each and all of them together. And he seemed to have found himself one new come friend in particular of a booze drinking sort with whom he imagined, with a no placed optimism, he would be able to come to better known terms with than most. The drinker of booze was an artist called Agnes Mortimer. She not only turned out to be a curious someone but one, he later discovered, who had much in finking common with his own gone self. And even though there had been an immediate look of long stared attraction between the two of them, the knowing burn was a slower one than most which could only grow at the pace that it would, not at their own minded choosing. Although, whether or not it could ever have been something which either of them were keen to choose or otherwise, was harder to know. It was, however, clear enough, to their friends and those who knew them, where an explanation for this might have been, as there was no looking about to be cushioned from the blurred edges of their own selves. In the same way as there were no expectations or a feeding of needs to be eased through the actual happening of their without fail, mutual turning up at the same almost arranged place, at the same almost arranged time. And even though this was held together with more of a reasoning lack than each of them could understand, it was so long way odd that the oddness itself was endearing enough to be seen, not least because Agnes Mortimer and Woller were known for only hitting their stride when the sun had fallen down, off to the side. Which meant that if their colliding and running in of bones was to continue, it would do so, either, in the latest hours of a night or during the earliest hours of a morning or later still, early on a following day, when after getting up from being sat on a wooden bench seat under a covering tree, the two of them might take a wandering turn in echo clacked shoes. And more often than would have been thought, the sitting and the taking of a wander were done with an absence of spoken words which were given over instead to a recognition of a like minded, long in the making, self. One that had become what it was through a slow pull rather than a hurtled push. As such, this had been a good thing for a pair as they were, for the time was better well used and not easily snatched or scratched at without the patience to know or even the verve to show just what could be learned as original fink. Agnes Mortimer had, well back and sometime before, enjoyed a peculiarly fleeting degree of moodling success as a member of a group of artists and finkers numbering seven in all, though, she had, quicker than the other six in a row, become less than more pleased to be included on a list of frowned on groups and individuals. Consequently, she had sudden time and quiet, found herself cut loose and replaced by a new drawn member about whom not much was known, either by her or anyone else. Worse was to come, when, in the wake of her own subsequent complaints, she had been left out in the cold without even being told about how she might have been just wrong enough to be removed in such a manner. She seemed to be free but aimless too, even in her better moments. Away from the people with whom she had thought, with whom she had smiled, with whom she had laughed, with whom she had talked, almost to the point of louder, hurl shouted words, she fought against the ease of being caught with a wrought handed feeling. On the inside of her own mind, Agnes Mortimer was well aware that when she had first seen a hint of a look from Woller, she was pulled up sharp with a frustrating turn as nothing which she could try would seem to work or to function as it ought, with almost all of it being stalled and close to falling broke. There even seemed to be a reasoning loss to the meaning as matter which was as rough and as torn as it was, loose held from whatever the essence of her work had for a long time been. And with more of a surprise than much else, it had at some point or other changed how she thought about her own sense of seeing, which was not the sort of change she wanted to feel, even though, it occurred to her that she was even less sure about her own need to control those changes which could come hurtling on in with no flicker of a warning, whenever and from wherever change came. Because of this, she wondered about the how of her work as much as the what, remembering when she had earlier thought that it could change everything until she became less than more sure it could change anything at all, as it seemed not to matter to anyone except to those who thought it mattered to everyone. No amount of bewildered goggling, however, had entirely convinced her to take a beaten step back from working in her own studio and although there had been and there continued to be some long, clock stretched moments of floor laid and ceiling stared, hardly seen means, she was determined to get on with as much of her own work as she could in her bare stood feet, just as she always had. Agnes Mortimer knew, deep in her own bones that whatever she might look at from the going moment on, she could not then see it again in the same way as she seen it before, as a new how to and a new want to were of coming importance now that something had changed. Although, whether or not the doing of it had changed her or she had pulled it into a well fitting shape of her own sort, was a question to which she did not have an answer. On the matter of their becoming a joined together pair with the finking relation of minded thoughts, as well as the occasional bed clambered sleeping between them, both she and Woller were glued, in the manner they were, as much around a shared careering heave as they were to their own selves. But whatever it was that the other had found in the finking and the clambering, it seemed only to confirm to each of them the constant presence of a keening need which was reckoned, by their friends and those who knew them, to be the weight of meaning where the personal, such as it was, could not exist in a condition of withdrawn isolation. And then Woller met Clementine Murnegan, coming across the ice, as the one collided with the other in the dark, on the frozen meadows of Whittlesey fen. The night was cold and star filled, as whatever feeling was hanging around in a lurk, waiting on a chance, took it with a quickening seep into their clothes, seeping right on through to the bones until the two of them, each and the other found themselves hurtling and skidding at a sliding run over the freezing gleam, headed in the direction of Clementine Murnegans black tin house, where the shirt fumbled, skirt dropped clambering was more and not less. And longer than most. Then in a sudden flash and with no hint of a shouted warning, he was out of the bed and trousered up smart, before legging it off in a clatter, down the stairs and away through the front door without being much clear even in his own mind about the why or the how or the where he was going. But because he did indeed seem to be going that seemed to be that. As he set off, though, on his foot stamped and arm flapped, cold breathing way over the fen with his back to Whittlesey, his loose hanging bones took a snap below his knees and rolled him fast into a ditch. When he woke up, it took Woller a longer while than he might have expected to realise that he could not make much of his own thoughts. Neither could he work out exactly where he was or just how he had got there at all, dressed, as he was, in a pair of blue pyjamas, while seeming to be laid out on his back in a wired, lighted and beep sounded bed of the sort which itself appeared to be different to any he had ever much been in before. At the same moment as he made an attempt to push himself up with his arms, so that he could get a better look at the room he was in, he noticed for the first time that there was a medicine man with a listening tube hung around his neck standing to one side of his own flattened out, blue wrapped self and looking down at him with, it seemed to Woller, a curious expression. Stranger still, this did not quite match the words he was then talking out loud, telling him, as he was that some hours before, he had been admitted to the small hospital in Thorney. This was, the medicine man said, because he had been taken sudden quick worse than ought to be thought, earlier in the week, when he had fallen hard on his head in a ditch. Woller said he could not remember doing the ditch falling thing and he asked how it was he had been turned up at the hospital instead of being left out cold in the open fen. But the medicine man simply creased his brow into a frown and replied that he had no idea about the how of it being done, only that done it had been. Woller was reckoned on asking him if he might know whether or not his condition was worse than ought to be thought. And so he did. But all the man with the listening tube hung around his neck would tell him was that he was sore enough to be there until he was either well enough to be discharged or noticed to be even worse off and long taken gone. Woller was left alone save for the better come feeling of a needle pushed deep into a vein in his arm, to fill up his brain with the morfiner juice which he was minded to think of as being a very good thing. It was quite some time later and not sooner, as he was sitting alone in his bed with the sheets pulled over his head, when, another medicine men came along and talking, told him that he was almost mended enough to be sent home. As this was as much as Woller needed to hear in his not much doing, foot up condition, it seemed a spurring moment to suggest that he was less than more sore than he was — enough to trouser up and shoe leg his bones out of the ward

and into the breathing air on the other side of the hospital
doors where he stood for a moment to gather his weight. And
to feel, clutched tight in a hand, his own new given package of
morfiner juice. On seeing him leaving, the medicine men and
the medicine women at the small hospital in Thorney had
collared his head with medical words and drummed it in on his
brain with more than less of a telling that when he had gone he
would need to take as much ease as he could, whenever he
could. Woller took them at their words, as he arrived back on
the inside of the cramped in small apartment at the School of
Thought, attached to Ayscoughfee Hall, crawling with a croak
of his own mattering means into the narrow bed. As he did so,
he thought it would be a good thing for him to not crawl back
out of it again for the better part of each day. And only then
when it became a necessary move to make. In spite of his
caution, the hurting pain continued to come at him, come for
him, catching him in the head, in the neck, in the eyes, in the
chest, in the stomach and in the bones of each shape and every
size. It caught him hard until he thought that there was not a
piece, not a part of him that did not hurt and that did not ache
or that would not stop chuntering at him from somewhere
under his skin. When a medicine woman came out to look at
him as he lay crawled in and curled up in his narrow bed,
sweating and shaking in his loosened bones, she talking told
him that whatever it was that was happening to him was only to
be expected for a man in his condition. And that he might as
well get himself used to it, for as long it would go on, however
long that might be. Although, *how* long it might be she could
not say, she said, as she bagged away her listening tubes before
leaving him to it, on the turn of a heel, through and out the
door of the cramped in small apartment. It seemed as though
the only thing he could do was to take the morfiner juice and sit
on a chair, be laid out in a bed or curled on the floor. Only

push it in and get it down to the spot. Just take the juice, the none more finer than the morfiner juice. Which he did. Without much knowing about it, his mind slowed to a dreaming speed, moving between sleep and otherwise, with the tale of Amos Cloot.

It seemed to Colonel Haw that the first thing (amongst all of the other things which were then caught in his brain) he ought to mention was that he had now started on a new and different sort of scribbled down work. With as much purpose as he could summon or as he said, in his own words, with a hurtling wallop, he was keen enough to explain the nature of the larger than otherwise confusions in which Meemo Leem was involved, from the number of talking words that he alone had talked about the cause of all the trouble. And it was there or somewhere about that he was aware of some sort of lack of understanding on the matter, on the part of some of those other than himself as it developed. He then thought that he ought to call on his own mind, in case he had forgotten about the time when he had had read through the whole of the history of the fennermarsh wars but then, if he had not, he was reckoned on wanting to let his own minded self know that one of the most remarkable episodes among the numerous others that could be recounted and held to be worth a favourable remark, was a clattering assault that was ordered by the clatterers from West Pinchbeck on those of a not quite the same sort from Crowland. This was made on the point of the geo featured logical end of the land before crossing to Pode Hole which took a spanning leap over the great stop, where some of the jacker booted clatterers were, in such a way that was less than good for them exposed to the shots on target of the hurl whacker guns of those in clatter come blue. The issue of which caused shouted and howled and bellowed out words, so that some of the clatterers lodged themselves on the whacking hurlers. And the main group made their own selves the keepers of the crossing point in the sudden come shoot without much of a game to be seen. Concrete and steel would be used for the purpose it had been decided before the leaping span, with much standing for the berserker slipping and the bongo slopping of the clatterers from the other side, who exposed each and all of a bone and a limb, calling in a come on to those who would take a shooting aim, to move them off and away from the where of their feet. Colonel Haw was reckoned almost certain that as this was the firmest cut of the haunch from the episode of which Meemo Leem was a boggle gone looker at the hop to Pode Hole, the mass of berserkers being cut off by the confluence from seeing much of each others operations, he was somewhat more eloquent and particular in his account of it. And the number of confusions he was in raised themselves up in his brain, straight out to what were, some would suggest, with an ease, the insurmountable difficulties he found in telling the words of his story with an intelligible (the shapes and the sounds and the colours of the wotchamacallit) voice while giving such clear made ideas of the various differences and distinctions between the zing and the zong and the bing and the bong and the boodler and the noodler, as to make those he might be with at the time understand just where and what it was he seemed to be on about. Colonel Haw was caught with a thought that it was often the case that scrawlers themselves were too apt to confound terms, so it would be the cause of much less than otherwise wondering if in his mufflehooned efforts to explain them and in opposition to more than a few conceptions of a missed sort that Meemo Leem did, in no time quick, boggle and puzzle those of his visitors who had not much expected to be boggled and puzzled. And sometimes, when the words were out too sudden and loud, he would find himself lost in them too. To speak it as plain as he reckoned it could be spoken or if Meemo Leem was in one of his best explaining moods, it was a soon gone difficult thing to keep the coursing of opinion free from turning up and off to the no way, long goner hoop. What rendered the account of the events more than less peculiar to Mister Lister was that in the clattering assault before the leaping cross, extending itself from the bank, on up to the great water stop, the ground was cut and crossed with such a patterning of channels and water on all sides that he would sooner than not get himself in such a sad, wonk kiltered state, set fast amongst them. So for some of the time, he was neither gotten on backwards or forwards to keep a hold of his breathing. And was, more often than most, obliged to give up the clattering assault for this reason alone. It was apparent to Colonel Haw that these keeling stoppers gave Meemo Leem more hard pulled frustrations than could be imagined, meaning he had a less than easy task of it. No doubt, he had a shoulder clamped hand on his own self and could make a much done deal on the matter of appearances but when he could not retreat out of the zing and the zong without getting into to the bing and the bong or get out of the boodler and the noodler without falling down the thingamajig, nor cross the leaping span without danger of slipping into the river below, he must have fretted and fumed deep down on the inside. Which he did. And these small but loud and much more than otherwise bellowings might have seemed of no account to the person who had not seen a well reckoned scribbled down work or a scrawled out version of the fennermarsh wars. A person, who had considered long, the effects which the enthusiastic gurning and the affectations of the mind might have had on the moogling of the gut. As such, it was not only on a froogler done thing. A spoongrease shoveller might sooner than not catch a thinker of what hooping jumps and sharp contortions of his wounded bones Meemo Leem must have gone through, under, over and down, on that score at least. Whenever Colonel Haw gave it a bit of a ponder, he was boffed in his brain with the realisation that it was a subject on which Meemo Leem could not come even close to pondering himself, reckoning, as he did that it was enough of a thing for him to feel it was so. And having been whacked hard with the hurting jabs and the clonking sots of it for a long time gone, he was determined to find some way or other to push out a reaching hand and raise his own self clear. It was at a point in the course of a morning, when Colonel Haw was taking a moment for a slow lie down on a floor of his own choosing that he was able to see, sudden time quick, just how the curious jagging and jongling wagging effect of the wounded bones on his brain had caused Meemo Leem such a clonk to his balance as to fetter him where he was. And therefore, in no position to be any other where than there. This was then followed when a second thought came into his brain that if he could get each of his hands on such a thing as a heavier in scale charted draw of the bigger gone stoppers over the leaping span, close to the goner big stop at Pode Hole, it might be a means of cutting a run and making a dash to throw a smash bashing line to Major Steel. And give him the means of a clattering chance. For no better reason other than it seemed to be, Colonel Haw was of an opinion that the attachment which Meemo Leem had to his wounded bones was because the wounding had come in one of the channels to the approach of the crossing leap of the thingamajig there. He was, therefore, more than less sure he could jab a finger without looking to see where, on the exact same charting of a rendered scale, of well drawn water, similar to where he might have been when the boomer struck him. All of this was as Colonel Haw had long time suspected it would be when collecting, for Meemo Leem, his wotchermacallit. Knowing him to be as minded as he was, there could be nothing so caught to be fraught when making an attempt of this sort to order things so much worse, to let the carpers from a platoon of the same name, swing a cracking blow and bring the whole of it down in a crash. As such, Colonel Haw saw it would be a better thing than not to watch out for both, as there were none to be trusted like some of them ought to be. Colonel Haw was also keening straight for Meemo Leem to tell the late arrived (it was slow, in the snow, they said) delegation from Throckenholt how much each and all of them were welcome, seeing as *each and all* of them were needed on the score which was soon to be accounted for with the regiment of opposing clatterers, sudden come from the wilder reaches of the eastern fen lands. It seemed to be a well handed card (he was neither a harper or a carper) to Colonel Haw that the people of Throckenholt were smack on the nose when the call to assemble a delegation rose in the open freeze of the eastern fen, as those who had been sent for and who had then come were of an excellent sort, being well accustomed to the violence of a clattering fight, each and all of them wanting for no courage or a berserkers mool – only to whistle the hooblayong. And of more than less than of a matter to Colonel Haw, it soon came to his attention that each and all of them, as one, were of the opinion of never having seen a scrawling work such as Meemo Leems own scrawled lines on the cause of all the trouble. Colonel Haw wondered what it was that was causing him to call out for cousin Wilomena whenever there was something to be given or something to be taken from someone or other, though, what, who or where, he was not so sure. With a curious line of running thoughts, it seemed that cousin Wilomena herself was closing on on a squealing bout. And then, when cousin Wilomena eventually decided to throw over the numbering claim, to loose off her leaving words like a flash from the start, she was a keener to snoogle a way on whichever chance there might be to gather the pieces and bits and parts of the brain, the grease and the squidge and the gristle of will, wherever and whenever it could be found. There might well have been nothing else which meant quite so much, thought Colonel Haw, other than for the author of the fennermarsh wars to give an understanding of what cousin Wilomena was gone in search of. And his long held and curious mind was not quite so done through that he was in need of being told, in the words of someone else, in words which were given out second about the mellergone means of it either. A sleight of a weighted hand from cousin Wilomena, looking too long for her spooning of grease and the search would be soon over and gone, goolon ool hot, goolon ool hot, as looping as a Sassa Quack. It was one reasoning way in which Colonel Haw could be seen to argue for a lessening of what was sudden quick becoming a series of events that were moving almost out of reach of speaking words, to whatever it was that could be turned out loose for the clattering to be done. With so much juice and so much bone to be lost, a well thinking fennermarsher could not consider them without a moment of easier caught hurt, deep in the flesh. What confusion from words of such meaning and odd sense, thought Colonel Haw, on the matter of the zing and the zong and the bing and the bong and not least the wotchermacallit. Without forgetting the boodler and the noodler, both of which were too hoola to be sure. When Meemo Leem had gotten his charted draw fast and deep in his mind, he started on in, with immediate effect, to turn his own self to the learning of it all over again, there being nothing of more importance to him other than the snort of the runner with soft worn shoes. With cousin Wilomena too, the meedling architect of some things which were good and some of a less so complexion, boomercumlingo, the fennermarshers tongue, was to form his conversation with a comprehensible sound. And before he was gotten even a short time along from the earlier gone start, he was straight off talking with words of more ease than a few and could make out not only the clattering of the the zing and the zong but having gone much deeper into the side than before, Meemo Leem was able to imagine a way across as far as the opposing clatterers line, to the leaping span at Pode Hole. And not least, he could then get a cautious hold on each of their fighting strengths. As to the weight of it, where he had earlier been whacked and cracked out hard with the wounded bones, each of them were his own. The more Meemo Leem looked over his charted draw, the more he could see his way to the how of a straightening leap, as Colonel Haw had reckoned he might, when he was free of the hauling of one form corruption or another. These could be a stopper on a crossing over the watered channels. And the river, a further hurl for which he had not quite then sorted out the means, though, he was convinced that there was a plan to be made for a clattering assault either with an earlier gone start or a later come ending. At some point around then, Meemo Leem had purchased a Quoodling edition and found that it was translated from the old gone form to a new and better version of the fennermarsh tongue. With one name after another, there were more than a few books of meedling opinions, as cousin Wilomena was found to have, on the history of the fennermarsh wars, when Professor Quiller and her assistant took a barging charge clean through some well rounded notions of a questioning mind. Towards the beginning of the soon to be ended gonnering slope, Meemo Leem found it necessary to understand a little of the how of the hurl whacker guns. And having reckoned it best to draw on what he might have, on the inside of his own ham crackered brain, he started with cousin Wilomena who, it seemed, to him, at least, could be the first person to be heard from, there and then, to have detected the inclusion of a new sort of clattering line. Cousin Wilomena had proved to Meemo Leem that she was an impossible girl with her carefree bawler of a way but he was, nonetheless, resolved in his own mind to find out which way a bawler could go, so he decided to set out with a moolas and watch her close. As he wandered along, where the history of the fennermarsh wars was supposed to have been scrawled out and down, he was sudden time pitched up close against either a hinner or else a honner, he could not be sure which on the whole line of approach to the leaper and the site of trouble caused deeds. With these having been done throughout the course of the episode, as it was (the billanong bellanang ballaloo) then, Meemo Leem took a sudden quick swipe without so much as a warning shout, to dismiss the given advice of Professor Quiller and instead, he bellowed at Major Steel to make sharp and get a jump on with some sort of doing on the matter of the crossing to be done at Pode Hole. And then, as if he was not in enough of a gloomer, he mumbled a grumble in the vague direction of where cousin Wilomena might be. Worse still, he began to lose most of the rest of his patience with the more often than some dependable Major Steel. As he heard the officers boots echoing out with a click and a clack along the length of the corridor that led to the where of the chair, in which he was sat, he threw down the forms (for the informing of and the informing on) he had been attempting to read and let loose a howling yell of shouting words about the urge of a need for a clattering leap sooner and not later than then, with the suggestion to Major Steel that such a thing might have been done at least by the time that each of them could see was now. And so it was agreed between the two of them, each and sort of the other that one more attempt would be made before the clatterers of the other side were of more in their number than were seen to be now. Cousin Wilomena was as struck by Meemo Leems words as Major Steel had been confounded, aware, though she was, of the corner to be fought, for the who and the what and the where of the clatterers bound on a common course. It seemed to be a clear enough thing to Meemo Leem, in his own mind, at least that he ought to hurl a farewell sound of the boomers booming even more and not less than before.

The sound of knocking on the outside of the door turned out to be coming from the knuckles of Thelonius Greeling, as he rapped Wollers mind into focus before walking through to the inside and sitting himself down on the chair which stood at the side of the bed. And then, he took a look at Woller in much the same way that all of those who sat on the chair that stood at the side of the bed did. Woller had never been sure about exactly what the look was but he was aware that it always looked to be the same. Thelonius Greeling talking, told him that he had been scrawling his hands and his brain to a worn out state and that he needed to clear off with his own self for a short while of some laid down rest in the Welney marshes, these being somewhere he reckoned he could be quiet. The water would be high at that time of the year and the sense of bleak isolation would be at its most insulating, with only the sounded conking of the swans to break the silence.

Clementine Murnegan was more than several weeks lost in
a confused daze of her own due to not having known where
Woller had gone when he had trousered up and legged it off,
down and out of her black tin house on the edge of Whittlesey,
on the day that he had. Such was the cracking in her own mind
about his sudden legging away without even a word of why or
what for that she had not been out through her own front door
in all the time since. She had not seen the looks or heard the
sounds of others in a lost number of weeks, only the look of her
own self in a mirror. And the noise of her own voice whenever
she made a squawk or spoke words out loud. Then with no
hint of a warning and as sudden as the hole had appeared, it
was closed tight again when Oscar Sollermon telephoned and
talking, told her about Woller and his hospital done stretch.
Clementine Murnegan thought it might be a fair reckoning to
make that whatever it was that had been enough to collapse
Woller into a ditch, was not because of her but because of his
poorly gone state. She, therefore, concluded that his earlier,
sudden legging it off had been the result of a quick time need
to get himself to a medicine man sooner and not later than
he could. And with this, she was close to bursting the seams
of her skirt with concern, along with a wanting to be near
him. In order to be there for his bed crawled means, curling
up from the resting core, she found and rented a house in the
same street, almost next to the School of Thought, attached to
Ayscoughfee Hall. This turned out to be a mistake of a thing
to have done. When Oscar Sollermon telephoned Woller and
talking, told him that Clementine Murnegan had pitched
herself up in the nearest house she could find and was needing
to see him, Woller bawled out in a furious hurler of shouted
wordss that it was not for him to be needed and not by her.
Woller then telephoned Clementine Murnegan and hurled the
same words straight at her, down to the end of the line, loud

in her ear. Not wanting to hear that she was far from a good thing but worse, closer to a bad thing, Clementine Murnegan gave in, bagged up and went back to her own black tin house on the edge of Whittlesey. Alone again, Woller crawled back in the narrow bed and laid his own means up with the intention of doing so for as long it would take to be done. Although even there, on his back and staring up at the ceiling for long gone reaches of time, he was oozed in his brain with flickering jabs of a rare sort of meaning. Unless, he thought, his brain had been jabbed with fleeting moments of forgetting about the who and the why and the how and the where and the when that he was. On the end of such thinking, he only knew he was not much keen on his brain being moved to forget or for him to become forgotten by those who might not even remember that they had done so. And searching through a haze of confusion and morfiner juice, he wondered what more there was to come for a bed crawled finker after a close run thing. What occurred to him then, with more of a surprise than otherwise, was that he seemed to be not much keen on being gone.

A quarter of the way through the second week of crawling in and out of his narrow bed in the condition he was in, Woller came to a sudden realisation that the feeling he had was better than the one he had before. And so he decided on clambering out of said narrow bed, trousering up, cramming a bag and clomping a boot out of the cramped in small apartment before legging it off to the Welney marshes in order to have a time of it at the gathering bash to he held by Thelonius Greeling, who had announced, to his friends and those who him, his need for such a thing now that he seemed to be mended in his own head. In addition to this, he reckoned there was a less than more knackered hang in the rest of his bones after a good enough time of doing nothing at all out in the open fen, amongst the willow trees and the conking swans seen flashing white in the greying skies, either side of flapping *down to* or *up from* the flooded marsh, honking, hissing, dipping and diving with long necked searching beneath the scum. He was minded to think out loud to blue eyed Basil that it had been these lean, sometimes quiet, hours along with the shortening days of the month which had been the only mending glue with sufficient stick to pull all of him together, in as good a shape as he could have hoped for; something he had been in need of well before he had come. As soon as the mending *was* over and done, it caught him clear in his thoughts about what he wanted to do. And this was to gather about him more than a few of those finkers who could be persuaded to boot a way out from Wisbech across the cut scarred land to the Welney marshes. Although, a notion such as this was easier to be thought than wrought for the simple reason that during his time there, Thelonius Greeling had made a home for himself in a place of a less than usual sort. This was not much more than a part fallen down, draught blown hut which sat low against the winds that came hurtling across the land from the eastern fens, cutting into the bones of all those who were caught in its path. A bare facing panel which served as both the front and the back door was badly hung and made of tin, causing it to clang, rattle and bang when caught, sharp and winded on its hinges. On the inside, there was not much to be seen in the way of comforting means for a gathering bash, other than a stuffing burst chair which was sat, angled sharp, at the foot of a large bed with three broken springs. Aside from these two pieces of furniture, there was nothing more than a bowl and a cup and a knife and a spoon. These were the sum of the items to be used on the inside of the part fallen down, draught blown hut in which Thelonius Greeling had been making the most of a heel kicked while. It was, therefore, more welcome than otherwise when a gathering bash was well enough done, with booze being found to be drunk down slow by those finkers who had turned themselves up. And in spite of the fact that he had been doing better than some to roll through a reeded drain with an old, torn boot, Woller could also be seen among the crowding boozers, though, how he had gotten himself there, he was less than more sure. As the booze was eventually emptied out from each and every one of the now hollow clanked bottles, it was thought that Thelonius Greeling was filled to the brim with celebratory joy when he announced, sudden time quick that the bash of a gather was over. On the follow of the night before, it was all he could do to take several wary steps through and out the door of the more than ever fallen down and open shell of a hut. With a push on each of his weighted feet, he got them into their shoes, to be stood with a sway, as he thought about how he could make a clomping way gone, back across the fen to Wisbech.

At the beginning of the second day in March, it occurred to Woller that he ought to be feeling quite a way better in his own bones than he was. On the other hand, he was minded to think of his condition as being no worse than it had been for some time, not least because he was now able to breathe in and out to an easier beat, with less than more of the aching hurt which had earlier been there. All of which he thought was a good thing. On the same day, however, he was caught up in a shouting slammer of a word hurler with Clementine Murnegan during which he shouted at her in the sharpest of words that he was calling it off on behalf of them both, each and the other, to end their together spent time before there could be more of it to spend. Whatever it was there had been between them that would be it, he said. This, he considered to be neither a good thing or a bad thing. It just was. Clementine Murnegan thought of her own self as the sadder of the two, though, she was, nonetheless, minded to hope for a saddened tear in him too, as Woller walked away without so much as turning around. When, on the following day, the one stumbled into the other in the road, the other suggested to the one that a last shoe kicked and skirt dropped, bed clambered fumble might be a thing to be done, if there was nothing else doing. It was and there was not. On this occasion, he hung about in a bed with her for three and a quarter days before making another of his sudden, not even hinted at, clearing off starts, being trousered up, down the stairs and out through the back door without a word of where he might go or for how long he would do so. Clementine Murnegan was quick on her feet but before she could move in a following dash, the sounded crack of the door against the frame of her black tin house told her that Woller was gone. Alone again with her own self, she walked around the fields in the gathering gloom for a number of scarce counted hours. The two of them, each and the other, in their own recent times, had made for themselves a name for a particular sort of shouted, foot stamped, hurled out bawler of a ding, dong, clonk, so, to their friends and those who knew them, such a recent time clonking was no more and no less of a surprise. What was known only to Woller in his own mind, was that his sudden, clearing down, out and off and away from Clementine Murnegan, had more to do with the coming of someone new. This was another woman, though, not much the same as the now familiar Clementine Murnegan, standing as she was, shivering in a sodden field, wet and muddied in the slanting rain, with one empty shoe dangling loose from her fingers, held low at her side. She pushed a shaking hand through her hair and wiped away, with a thumb, the water from her eyes.

The reasoning that Woller had been doing for his careering sake had shoved him into a decision that if he were to become a more than less authentic finker of his own made brand, then he would need to let go of at least one element from his mattering means. In line with this, he therefore scrawled down a note on a piece of paper which he then left, pinned on the outside of the door, of his cramped in small apartment, at the top of the stairs in the School of Thought, attached to Ayscoughfee Hall. The noted scrawl was not addressed to anyone he knew, to a member of the faculty or even to the school. He had simply and in not so many words, given immediate notice that he had decided it would be better not to continue with his work as a researcher at the school; and that he would be gone from the building with as quick a stride as he could make. And so he was. It was only at a time that was later and not sooner than his up and leaving, off and out of the school and the cramped in small apartment that it kicked home in his brain, in an occurring way, to Woller that he would then need to find himself another place in which he could heel off his shoes on the floor, on the inside of his own front door. He wanted, was well aware that he needed, a house which would be a home of his own. A house in which he could be who he was when he could not be seen either by his friends and those who knew him or by those who weren't and who did not. Whatever there was that could be claimed by him, he wanted it to be there and not elsewhere, boxed in and damp in warping piles, stacked to a height in the cornered gloom of a room that was not his to be seen. And with or without a reasoned think, he knew that the thing he wanted and had wanted long time gone and more, was a piano on which he could play. One on which he could glide and in which he could hide from whatever it was that he needed to be hidden, whenever it might be that he did. At this, he could feel a widening tear at his not once having had a piano that was his and only his, for the playing and the gliding and the occasional self gone hiding. And even though he did not have much to show for one other than his worn through pockets full of holes, the possibility of his showing up for one at the piano sellers practice rooms which were set aside for the comers and getters of the sounded notes, was something he was caught with in a hold. In his own minded way, he wondered at the how and the why of his never before having a home that he had ever thought of as being his. Somewhere he could not be moved on from, moved off or moved out without his own wanting to be gone. Wondering if this were really the case, he gave it a good remembering go. But still, he could not call to the front of his mind a time of much longer than weeks or months that he had spent in a shoe heeling state on the floor, stretching his face with a smiler on the warmer of his own front door. And he was beginning to reckon that he could not do any of the finking work he wanted to do, as he could not pull anything out from a big eared hat or feel secure in his own self until he had found such a place for his own self to be. A home finking home which was his. There was, however, a stopper on his starting to do less than little about it that he not seriously considered before then. It caught him with a crack in the head of a minded sort that sooner and not later, he ought to consider the way in which he would find himself sat down on the floor, on the inside of a house that belonged to no one else but him. Confused about much, he wondered what he been thinking. Of all the things he could have considered, he had forgotten to consider that which he ought to have scrawled down in a dark red ink at the top of a list. Worse, though, than this, was a realisation that obliged him to draw the most important, unfortunate conclusion, as far as he was concerned which was that he could not even begin to be cashed up enough to afford a heel kicked, shoe dropped, home of his own. At least, the not moving without wanting to be moved sort that he wanted. This gave him a done in feeling and he kicked at one of his feet with the other in some annoyance before then deciding to curl himself up in a huddle, inside his coat and push himself as deep into a doorway, in a building, on a side street, running off a main street, as far in as he could get. After a short head scratch, he thought it might be better if he stayed where he was and only stand himself up again back in the side street when he knew that he could be minded enough to accept the making of a choice. One that was less than much of the kind he would otherwise have chosen to make. And so he did. After some time curled and some time stood, staring out, pulling at his hair and rubbing at his chin, he started looking again for a place in which he could be on the inside and not on the outside. A place in which he could take out his books from their mouldering old boxes. A place in which he could heel off his shoes. And where he could not be moved without his wanting the moving to be done.

After what he reckoned was less than more of a while spent wandering through the streets in the opposite direction to the one he might have taken earlier before, he found himself brought to a slow walking pace by what he thought could be a part of town to be considered as somewhere to make a lasting home. This was a new comer quarter of Wisbech which was then filled to the burst with those who had come from wide across the fen lands in search of something other than whatever it was each and all had chosen to leave behind them, wherever it might have been. As a crowded, boisterous choice for a home to be made, it could, thought Woller, give some oomph to his bones, with a whirl of continual change which saw people, ideas, furniture and food moved through and about the streets and houses there – some of which bore echoes from a long gone earlier association with the docks in the town. And in spite of it being a worse done part of town than elsewhere, there seemed to be a shared endeavour among those who could be seen in the sellers of goods and the numerous spoongrease dinner shops which were also to be found, crammed full, as they were, with a teeming mass of spooning guzzlers. To his surprise, Woller was quick time caught in the brain with a sudden whack that it was there and it was then, as he stood where he did and looked about him, at the place he found himself in, knowing this was the where and the when that he wanted to be. But more than all that and better than ever, was the thing on which Woller was most keen. This being that some of the new comer quarter was an emptied out shell, sitting useless and silent and hollow. It was understood, by those who made it their working while to understand that for a home looking stumbler to get themselves through and in the door of their chosen stack of bricks was a matter as simple as the cracking of a lock. Woller was big time wanting to know how this might be done, so with this in mind, he thought about asking those he saw standing in or sitting on or walking along or running through the streets, for advice, in order for him to be expertly learned a good lock cracking technique. As much as he was keen to learn, however, he was also less than otherwise pleased to realise that if he *were* to ask those he had seen, in a stand, on a sit, along a walk, through a run and about for an idle in the streets, such a question as that then the who and the where and the when and the what of the why he was there in the new comer quarter would be known further out than in just his own brain. This, he reckoned, would not be a good thing. And so, instead of opening his own mattering means for others to see, he decided to leg up his feet and wander off in search of a quieter patch where he might find himself a house with a lock to be cracked. And so he did.

Woller had wandered only a short time and a shorter way from the busier, noisier parts of the new comer quarter when out of the corner of an eye, he caught sight of what he had been hoping to find. As he stood and looked on at what he was beginning to think of as his new home, it was easy enough for him to see that it was a house as odd as the street in which it was stood, being, as it was, a narrow, four storey, brick built town house that had been painted on the outside in a colour that was a sort of green and a sort of grey, at the same time as seeming to be not much of either. While the doors and the windows had been painted in a colour that was a deep grey, almost black which sat, flat against the sort of green, sort of grey but not much of one or the other colour of the bricks. He did not need to pull a frowning stare too hard to notice that not a single window was of the same shape or of the same size as the other windows or that there were three, apparently identical, front doors in a row which fronted the street. Woller was intrigued by the notion and also by the lollabong thinking of the mind which had, whenever it had, been minded to place three of the same front doors in a row, at the front of the house. The why of it was something that threw his head in a reel. Then as he stood where he was, sort of staring and sort of hum ha harring, on the reasoning of the teaser, he realised there was more he could do. And in a sudden quick flash, he had taken a lurching hop on his toes, with a clatter of his bones, into the door that was furthest to the left of the other two. He reached out a hand and pushed down on the handle with a tentative turn which to his surprise, turned, allowing him to pull the door open and away from the wall. But he was bewildered to find that rather than looking through to the inside of the house, all he could see was a wall of bricks built fast into the wooden frame. It seemed to be a made on purpose stopper that could be opened but which could not be come through or be gone through by whom so ever was on the outside, trying to get to the inside. Confused, he scratched at his head and stood for a moment to stare at such a bonkers done thing, before closing the door against the wall. Stepping over to the same looking door in the middle, he pushed down a reaching hand on the handle of that one too. Again, it turned but this time the door opened inwards, as he held it, causing him to be pulled in, only catching a hang on the frame with his other hand, so as to break his own fall. Although he had almost gone for a slight topple and down, Wollers feet were still where they had been on the street, on the outside of the door which he considered to be a good thing, as he was less than more keen on going through it to the inside of the house when he had not taken a look at whatever was behind the third door in the row. Closing his eyes, he made a toe lurching hop to one side. And then he stood where he landed without moving, hoping he would be where he had intended to land, while also not being able to decide in his own mind if he wanted to know what was behind the number three door. Would it be the same or would it be different to what had been on the other side of door number one and door number two? Hum ha, he thought, hum ha indeed. After a quiet think, with one of his fingers jabbed in one of his ears as a help, he concluded that it would be better to know than not. And so he first opened one eye and then the other, to stare hard down at his shoes which were at just such a well placed pace from the outside of the number three door for him to reach the handle in one go with his right hand. Managing to keep a loose hold, he gave it a downward push. With no hint of a warning, the door swung open and outward into the street without even the need of his pulling it toward him, causing Woller to take a jumping step back on his heels to avoid a clonking knock as it did so. When it had stopped its swing and simply hung, as if it had been flung to one side on its hinges, the number three door could be seen to be of an almost identical make to the number one door, over to the far left, next to the number two door in the middle. As he stared again, as he had done twice before, Woller was not quite as surprised as he might have been had he not already seen a similar thing a few moments before, to see a wall of bricks blocked up fast in the frame. As far as he could tell, the only difference between either end of the walls of bricks was that the one in front of which he was standing was not as plain as the first, there being seven bricks which were painted alternately in a pale cream and a sage green. Woller reckoned this to be more than less anticipated, as he stood, rubbed at his chin and ran one of his fingers over the seven painted bricks in the vague hope that the touching of them might make the reasoning of it clearer than it then was. It did not. Although, he thought of this as neither a good thing nor a bad thing. It was simply an odder thing than not. And that was fine with him. With a shouldered heave, he managed to swing the number three door shut, back where it had been against the wall. Then he stood for a moment to ponder on the curious happening of the doors as each of them were, as there seemed to be a reasoning lack for them all. And there quite evidently could, in the minds of those who might be standing out in the street, hoping to knock their knuckles on the appropriate door, be some confusion. Woller thought of this as being a good thing. As he continued to stand where he was, looking at the house, he could see that although it was more than most, a peculiar place, the street of eight houses in which it was stood was no less so in the way that it had been strangely laid with no apparent design or plan. It could even be seen in a blink that of the other seven houses in the street, there was not a single one which appeared to be the same shape or of similar size. Some of them were extraordinarily tall and some of them were astonishingly small, showing not much height above the top of a door. Of the other seven houses in the street, not one looked to be of a facing line that was less or more wide or narrow than the next one along. And each of the other seven had been constructed in different ways and with different means, variously built using cut wooden planks, shape hammered tin, plastic from moulds and plastic in sheets, old copper plate, concrete in blocks and glued together straw. And of the other seven houses in the street, each had been sited at a slight angle to the next one along or been slotted in a shorter distance forward or a longer way back. Woller reckoned that the mere sight of such a street would stretch a beamer of a smile over the face of those who might be stood there to see it. Although, whether anyone else, other than him, could see it in quite the way that he did as a place in which he could heel off his shoes and set down his loose hanging bones for good, he was less than more sure. What he did know was that his shoes, his clothes and his bones would be almost all there was to be found on the inside of the four storey town house with the three deep grey, almost black, painted front doors, if it were to become his. There would be nothing to be sat on or laid out in, other than the floor, because there had not ever been anything of his to be owned. Even so, he did not consider this to be much of a problem, as he reckoned he would be happy enough to sit down on the floor for sitting and to lay himself out on it for sleeping, with only the vaguest of half thought notions that he would do this until he had a chair on which he could be sat. And a bed in which he could sleep. Again, he looked at the house, as he stood where he was. `With a glance at the other seven houses in the street before staring down at his feet and then at his hands, he held them up to his face to see if they and his mattering means were there, where they were, at the time and in the place he thought it all was. As it seemed to Woller that everything was as well it could be, he took a walking step forward and stopped in the open doorway of the house which was almost his new heel kicked home. Leaning his head just through into the entrance hall he sniffed a slight sniff and then held in his breath as he waited for his nostrils to contract and his brain to melt, before leaking out through his ears. When sooner and not later he realised that neither the contracting nor the melting had happened, he drew in a deeper breath that filled his nose with a smell that smelled of nothing. There seemed to be no lethal keeler to be had. As a sense of relief swept through his bony frame from the hair on his head to the tips of his shoes, he turned on a heel, went inside and closed the door.

At the beginning of December, it had all of a sudden become an obvious enough thing to his friends and those who knew him that there was a new and conspicuous presence in Wollers life. A different someone, who seemed only to have appeared at a time when she had been least expected to do so, by both him and them. The first time Woller had met Catherine Cole, she had talking told him that she was better than any other finker had ever been or would then be. Better than all the rest of his friends and those who claimed to know him. There were no squealers more admiring of his work or more understanding of him and his mind. She was, she said, as familiar with that which he had done as he was himself, claiming too that her own reading of the finking scrawl by the various finkers from the established cultural elites of Gosberton Clough and Tydd Gote was wider and deeper than many of those whom he might have known. Some of whom could have read no more of it than she had. She also made a promise that no matter what Woller might scrawl or what he might think, she would give him her own minded thoughts on it all which would be keener and better than most. Then she said that sometimes at moments she never knew before she did, her mind loosed off barely thought notions which turned into words and actions that could spin out, crashing into those who might be close enough to be crashed in on. Woller thought of this as a strange enough confession but not necessarily a bad thing. Then Catherine Cole talking told him that she had a piano of her own, even though it was elsewhere until she could find somewhere for it to be. Somewhere for it to stay and for it to be played by someone who could. This seemed to Woller to be an exceptionally good thing.

Although Catherine Cole had crashed in on Woller without much of a hinted warning, she was more than less keen on hanging around, knowing as she did that with such a keener as she on his hands, he would be less than more concerned about seeing Clementine Murnegan again. And however he had been with her and whenever he had been it which had been often, Clementine Murnegan found herself to be of the same minded wanting as he was. Although, even as it was, whatever it was, it was not thought to be a keeper, either by their own selves or by their friends and those who knew them, all of whom considered the time to be going, sooner and not later. The time that *was* spent and the times that *were* had by both Woller and Clementine Murnegan with each and the other were desperate and bruised, given over to the brittle amusement of staying awake in her bed in her black tin house for days on end, drinking down booze – and taking a hollow eyed share of his morfiner juice. At other times, the times that were had were spent walking for hours through the streets, along the tops of the wide cut drains and over the fields, ambling, scrambling, trudging and wading, each of the two of them in rubber boots, longing for rain. And she, clinging on to her own thinking that at some point sooner and not later they could, each with the other, make something bigger and more smiling out of their being together, though she only thought such things. And he could not understand that which she would not say.

After a hurl of persuasive words from Woller at a moment when she had been not much expecting them, Clementine Murnegan agreed to consider a suggestion of his on a collecting matter. As a well known collector of collectable shapes, she could most often be thought to be curious about the possibilities of something that might be a new thing, even if the something might not be a thing of any value. Whatever it was that Woller wanted Clementine Murnegan to see and to be caught in the brain with a collectors kick, was, at least for her, an intriguing distraction from the recent thoughts she was minded to think. The shapes would be seen. On the day, however, they could only be looked at with a smile, as the maker who made made them was in attendance, watching close whom so ever it was who was doing the looking. It had become obvious enough that green eyed Gertie was pleased with her own handed attempts at shape making. And because she never failed to assume that others would be of a similar opinion, she had not, for a moment, realised that what Woller was interested in was not her work but her. Consumed with her own making means, she often forgot she was there, wherever there or the time might be. So whenever those she took a look at looked back at her, green eyed Gertie was less than more sure that she could also be seen by them. A peculiar woman indeed, thought some. The works she had made were of a form that was hard to discern, while the colour was harder still with no obvious reasons for being either which neither Woller nor Clementine Murnegan could easily ignore. Although, in the circumstances, both of them made an effort to do so. Clementine Murnegan quick time realised that the shapes in question were questionable at best but she could not haul herself in from wanting to do whatever it might take to make Woller a smiler for her and for real. And so she agreed to a cash handing over for the entire collection, with the intention of putting it under a hiding

lock. Then, with a reasoning lack of a sort, she asked green
eyed Gertie if she would like to see where her work would be
placed. When green eyed Gertie said that she *would* like to see
where, Clementine Murnegan talking, told her this would be
at her house out on the Wash, at Dawsmere. As the Wash was
the place where the flat, scarred fen lands were brought to a
slow merging end by the sea, Clementine Murnegan was caught
with the thought that as such, there was much to commend it
to a would be hider of a poorly shaped collection. And because
it was also the only place with space enough for her to be a
lone sack of bones and mattering means, there could even be
a coming to terms with her recent bought shapes, given the
time to look and to think. She had taken no one else out to
the house before then but she reckoned that taking green eyed
Gertie might ease her own mind and Wollers too, into wanting
to be there for a longer come time.

The house at Dawsmere sat alone against the flattening winds, some way off from the other houses in that part of the fen, of which there were less than a few. As a home for Clementine Murnegan, it was old and pale, with a high wall around it which appeared to be older and paler still, the weakening stone here and there crumbling, the tumbled pieces lost in the long grass and the small wild flowers that grew at the foot of it. The house and the wall had been at an earlier time than then, painted in a particular colour, though whatever that colour might have been, it could no longer be seen on the windows or the front door or the back door or on the big wooden gates that sagged low on their hinges in the wall. With one gate long before swung open and at a slight angle to the other. In open spite of the winds that could flatten a standing person down on the ground as they hurtled in off the sea and over the fen, there were trees to be seen stood all around the old pale house, on the outside of the older and paler still wall. And on the inside of it too. There were short trees and there were tall trees, apple trees and oak trees, willow trees and sycamore trees, birch trees and beech trees, each of them rooted deep in the earth against being moved. As the three of them, Clementine Murnegan, green eyed Gertie and Woller stood in the garden, in the long grass and the small wild flowers under the trees, on the inside of the old and pale, partially crumbling stone wall, each of them were caught in the ears with a low gone sound. One of almost nothing to be heard other than the sound of the wind. A near quiet that was occasionally pierced with a shriek from a seagull wheeling high in the air, blown landward from over the sea. And because it was a lighted thin and cold fen stark afternoon late in the month, the air was sharp on their breath, as each of the three of them stood without moving and without speaking, only listening. Then, as quick as they had stopped, they were moving again with a soft footed tread around the garden to the back of the house, to the back gate, through which they could, when they looked, see the sea, rolling, breaking, grey green in colour, flecked with white foam. And sparkling with the fleeting light. But there was more to be seen than to be heard from where they were stood, the three of them in a row, with the only sound reaching their ears seeming to be a muted, sounded pounding of falling water on hard, wet sand. As the cold began to turn colder and a freezing chill came slicing in straight off the water, leaving the damp to be felt, seeping in through their coats and into their bones, Clementine Murnegan was about to suggest that they give up on standing out in the wind, when, in a quick, sharp flash of his flailing arms and his legs, his feet and his hands, Woller tore off his clothes before hurtling off, through the grass, across the mud, out over the sand and into the sea. He could be seen for a moment and then he was gone. Then, again he was there, in his now mottled skin, fleshed bright against a heaver of the darkening swell. The two of them, Clementine Murnegan and green eyed Gertie, the one and the other, were now standing closer in to the water looking on as he slipped under and over the surf, sometimes pitching up and at other times lurching through the waves, heading out deeper and further from where their feet were stood, half sunk down in the wet mud. In less than even a short while, he seemed to have swum so far out in the water that those on the shore, hard watching and soft mud sinking in each of their shoes, could not see him at all – the two of them beginning to think that he might not be coming back. Lengthened minutes seemed to creep by as the sea rolled and the sea broke, the foam sparkled in the fleeting light and the sound of the waves pounded the one and the other in their ears. And still, all they could see was the sea. Then sudden time quick, Woller was heaved up through a snorter of a white wave which hurled him out and thumped him down flat, beached, bruised and

retching on the sand. When he had stood himself up, he ran
over and back to where both Clementine Murnegan and green
eyed Gertie, the one with the other, were then pulling each of
their shoes out of the sucking mud and looking at him for the
berserker he might be taken to be. Woller, though, seemed only
to have been charged in his brain from his own gone loop in the
freezing water. Clementine Murnegan and green eyed Gertie
were, however, both of the same mind, being not much inclined
to share with him his somewhat alarming, charging and less
than ever predictable way of moving. All of this was the cause
for a catch in the words which were spoken as each of the three,
stood in the long grass by the gate at the back of the house, two
watching as one warmed himself up in his sea cold skin, under
trousers, jumper and coat.

Woller was surprised in his own mind when he decided to bring to a stop whatever it was he was continuing to do with Clementine Murnegan, while being less than more sure about the when and the how and the where, he thought he ought to do it. What he thought he *could* be sure of was his own knowing interest in the wonderful words and the startling thoughts of Catherine Cole more than those of Clementine Murnegan, only some of which he could continue to see as he had earlier done. It appeared to be obvious to his friends and those who knew him that it was Catherine Cole who had called him away from wherever it was he had been going before then. And even though he had been on the go, in a wandering way, he would at least have been gone, to have found himself to be somewhere, wherever that could be. Whether or not this would have been a good thing or a bad thing was not something he could know.

Woller was caught with concern that he might have drunk down too much of the booze. And pushed in too much of the morfiner juice, clambered too much, in too many beds and cared less than enough for his finking means. Although, he wondered with a harring hum, he might not have drunk down *enough* of the booze, not pushed in *enough* of the morfiner juice, clambered *too little* in *too few* of the available beds and cared *too much* for his finking means. Scrawling out words about the need for forthcoming means to matter more than less in his own knowing time, he could be seen to be hoping for something other than all that was gone. As such, he was minded to think that this was a question which was bigger than just him. And so he sent it to Oscar Sollermon, who replied that he had less of an understanding about the coming means to matter than Woller had himself. And whether or not he thought it would be better than some other mattering means was not an answer he could give him, so he gave him no answer of any sort, keeping whatever it was that he might have said on the inside of his own head. Woller thought that although a response of this sort from Oscar Sollermon would do nothing to ease his confusion, it seemed to become less than more important as a gradual realisation seeped into his own brain that his friends and those who knew him and also their friends and those who knew them, were bagging up and foot, shoe, legging it out of Wisbech in several different directions at once, each direction being taken because of convenience rather than choice, such was the hurrying to leave. Some of the legging finkers were heading for the more southerly smiles of Deeping St. James, while several of the westerly wingers were bagged up and heading for Sutterton marsh. As for the other finking footers who were going to neither of those, most were heading off for somewhere that was elsewhere to the place they were in. Woller was knocked with a wobbling bead by the going in all

directions of hurtling, finking sorts, not least because none of
them would make a break in their quickening stride to explain
to him why it was they were going, when, earlier gone, not one
of them had shown much interest in doing so. Attempting to
overcome the beading wobble, he reckoned that whatever the
reason for their striding was, he needed to know about it sooner
and not later. The one person he could find, who was not in
some sort of a rush and who would stay still for long enough
to listen to his spoken words was Clementine Murnegan. But
even she, when he asked her, was less than more sure of the
cause of the legging panic. Worse than this, she said, she could
not decide where to put her own mattering means in the
circumstances, whatever the circumstances were. Clementine
Murnegan looked at Woller. And Woller looked at Clementine
Murnegan. But neither of them, each or the other, could think
of what they might say or do to make sense of the moment
the two of them were in. Then Clementine Murnegan startled
both her own self and his by breaking the silence with a sudden
laugh that stopped as soon as it had laughed itself out, though,
it brought a look of surprise to her eyes, as she looked at Woller
who was stretching a smile over his teeth, as he looked back at
her. She talking, told him that it was no smiling matter but this
only caused him to laugh too which brought a smile to her face,
as she looked back at him. She then said that if she were to bag
up and leg it fast out of Wisbech, she would consider heading
across the fen to Surfleet Seas End, though, she also thought,
hum ha vaguely, about pointing herself in the direction of
Dowsdale where she could maybe make a start on sorting out
her own, almost forgotten, going to seed arrangements there.
She scratched at her head and stared out at Woller. She rubbed
at her chin and looked down at her shoes but Clementine
Murnegan could not reach a decision about what she thought
she ought or ought not to do, well knowing as she was that the

notion of ought was something she had never much liked. And so, for an apparent lack of anything to be done which could be reckoned by her to be worth doing, she simply sat where she was, in a state of sudden come stillness, in a chair, in the kitchen of her black tin house on the edge of Whittlesey. A bottle of booze clutched tight in her hands.

During the last few days of the month, the temperature dropped down low, lower even than was usual for the end of December. And on both the outside and the inside of more than most of the houses throughout the fen lands, the air began to feel colder than it had, glove and hat chillingly so, cutting under scarves, through sweaters and into those foot stamping, hand clapping fennermarsh people who could be seen skittering about on the frozen earth. Woller pulled a blanket around his shoulders, over the top of his coat and spent more than less of a while kicking time in its heels, sitting at whichever table offered a spare chair in whichever spoongrease dinner shop was the least crammed to the walls with other foot stamping, hand clappers, looking to get in to the warming feel, with the intention of larding up their ribs against the cold. As he sat, pulled close on a chair at his share of a table among the slowly warmed, steaming bodies of the grease shovelling crowd, he found himself listening to the spoken words to be heard around him, learning that for each and all, an approving look was something which had become more important than ever before. It seemed to Woller that it would, therefore, be sensible enough to make certain of his own status as a well approved finker. Although, he was less than more sure as to how this could be done. Hum ha, he thought. At the same time, Clementine Murnegan eventually arrived at a decision of her own which she considered to be neither sensible or otherwise, being nothing more than a point she had reached. And the point was, she talking, told Woller on the end of a telephone line that if, in the circumstances, there was less than small sense to be made of most of everything else, then she reckoned it would better to do what she did best – throw as many woozing parties for as many boozers as she could. And so she did.

A quarter of the way through the seventh day in April, a realisation turned over in Wollers brain that he ought to put in some scrawling time on the work in progress. So he pulled up a chair to his desk and sat himself down in order to make a start on the white, papered pages. The problem was, the white papered pages only stared back at him, as he stared at them, even though he knew well enough that he would need to be sat there, on the chair, at the desk, for most of each day, on more days than fewer, until it had become apparent that his scrawling words had taken on a form with which he could be pleased. And he also knew that there would be times when the scrawl would not move one way or another, either calling him close with an urge to bellow or swerve out the way whenever it seemed better to do so. With this in his mind, he decided to walk. And so he did, becoming lost in his own minded thoughts for eight and three quarter miles each day. At the end of a period of scarce remembered hours of long time scrawling, with the chairing, the desking and the staring, not to mention the wearing down of his first done notes, it seemed to Woller that the piece was complete. When he sent the manuscript out to a publishing pair in Dowsdale, both of them, together, looked at the sudden come parcel which was held in their hands before deciding to send it straight back with an immediate no. The two of them then locked the door and hid under a table. Woller dropped a line to Cornelius Karp who was away from it all with an overwhelming bout of lethargic means, though, he did suggest another publisher who turned it down too, barricaded the door and jumped out of the window. Ha hum, thought Woller, not for the first time.

A new finking opportunity that was more surprising than some came careering along on a cold blown morning to haul Woller out of a floor laid, ceiling stared daze, causing him to be sat straight up with a starting bang in response. What it was that was new and opportune, involved the scrawling finkers at a quarterly cultural review which had a distribution throughout the wider fen lands. This was edited by Silvester Guillory, who was, more than most, keen on all of Wollers finking works, reading whatever he could, whenever he could, wherever it could be found. Consequently, he telephoned Woller and asked him if he could possibly turn himself up for a speaking word or two, when he could find the time. Woller said that he could. And so he did, turning himself up in curious mode, through the door to the office of the quarterly cultural review to find Silvester Guillory hopping about from one of his feet to the other and waving his hands around in the air, seemingly unable to keep much of his own means still. As strange as it was to be greeted in such a manner without even sharing a spoken word, Woller thought he had seen stranger things in his own minded time. And besides, he was keening to know more about a hop, waving man who could either be excited to see him or was only doing what he did, no matter who was there or where he might be. Maybe he was a man who felt the cold more than most or was a poorly man or a madder man than some. Whatever the reason for a man to go hopping about from one of his feet to the other, it was a personal thing, Woller thought and not, therefore, much to do with him. So he stood where he was and looked at Silvester Guillory, who, sudden time quick, with no hint of a warning, stopped, right on the spot, whispering words about how he was honked out knackered with the editing life and wanted to retire on his feet while he could still use them. Woller was caught in his brain and astonished again when Silvester Guillory then said he would be happy to pass on his editor's pen to him there and then. It was a simple question, he said. Would Woller be interested in taking over as the chief editorial wheezer? There would, of course, be a small amount of self pocketed cash on offer and Silvester Guillory would arrange for the venture to be financed for as long as it could reasonably be expected for him to do so. Then he said that although he was making a sincere offer, he knew well enough that sincerity did not always win when losing was a possibility. And so, if Woller was not much of a fancier of the editorial wheezing, he would understand if his answer to the question was a no and not a yes, as he had hoped. It was a no, said Woller, explaining as best he could that taking over a quarterly cultural review was not the sort of opportunity he needed to career him forward as a finker. Worse, it could be one to pitch him over to wherever it was that Silvester Guillory appeared to be heading, on his sometimes hopping feet. This would not be a good thing, he said. As he looked at Silvester Guillory, he was quick time kicked in the brain with an overwhelming need to run, to show off his soles and break some speed, to put some space between his bones and the occasional waving hopper. And so he did, turning back through the door of the office and down the stairs, hurtling out into the street and running off, back home to his narrow, four storey town house, with the three deep grey, almost black, painted front doors.

Woller decided in his own minded way that he was much in
need of a place to escape from it all, to be alone in his creaking
bones, somewhere that was elsewhere. It, therefore, seemed to
him, obvious enough that a clean heeled bolter might head off
in the direction of Skeldyke for as long as a bolting heeler could
take it. Although, it occurred to him that even if he *were* to bag
up and foot, boot it off across the fen and over to the marsh, he
was not as well cashed up as he wanted to be. This was most
definitely a bad thing, he harrumphed, as he sat down on the
stairs in the hall. Looking at the inside of the one actual deep
grey, almost black, painted front door for inspiration, it was
clear that before he got up and went through it, he ought to
think about what he might do when he had done so. At the end
of a long moment, he settled his mind on a thought that he
reckoned was a practical one which could, sooner and not later,
lead to him becoming as cashed up as he needed to be. He
thought he ought to give serious consideration to becoming a
moodler. Although this was not something after which he
would ordinarily be keening, he understood that it could be
worth it in terms of the cash in his pockets, knowing, as he did,
that Oscar Sollermon had moodled his way out of a cash gone
crisis, whenever a cash gone crisis had turned itself up which
had been often. And even though he was less than sure about it
all, on further considered head scratching and chin rubbing, the
idea began to take on a will of its own, leading him to reckon
that Skeldyke could be the place to start on in as a moodler.
When, eventually, he turned his own loose hanging bones out
to the edge of the marsh, at the point where the fen became a
seeping, leaking, sinking morass which sucked down boots and
legs, up to a chin, a shriek and over a waving arm, slurping over
the top of a head before belching out a finishing glop, the light
was beginning to fade. On the follow of his pointing toes, he
took a slowing path of coarse grass through the vaguely salty

smelling boot slurper that stretched out on either side of him as he walked. That the wind, breezing in over the marsh from the sea, was not as flattening as it often was, allowed Woller to walk straight up, rather than leaning into and against it in an effort to keep moving forward. Even so, it was still fen stark and cold. A day for neck wrapped scarves and for glove clapped hands to beat off the freezing air. In the greying sky, geese flapped and honked their way over his head as he stood where he was, listening as the flapping of their wings became a quieter hum, the further away from him they went, until they specked in the distance and then vanished into the horizon. After a further mile or so of walking, slipping and sometimes foot splashing through the occasional running creek which bisected the path, Woller arrived at a small wooden shack. Standing out at the front of what would be his home for the coming weeks, looking at what could be seen of it in the approaching dark, he could see that it evidently was a shack, not much more and not much less. The outside of it was painted white and a single door was shedding peels of faded blue paint, some of which had peeled right off and were lying on the ground like fallen blue leaves. Up on the rusting tin roof, a wonky brick chimney leaned off to one side, while there appeared to be no more than three windows, each of a different size and shape. At the front, there was a large, rectangular window. At the side, to the left, there was a small square window. And at the back, there was a long, narrow window frame which ran along most of the length of the wall that made up the back of the shack. On closer peering, Woller realised that although there was no glass in the long, narrow frame, there was instead a row of empty glass jars, stacked along the sill where a window might have been. Walking back around to the front again, he went in, through the peeling, blue painted door to the inside, only to be stopped where he was, stood for a moment in the doorway, warily smelling the air for the lethal keeler that would do him in quicker than he could get out of the way. When he could smell nothing much to be scared of, he relaxed his lungs into an easier breather of calm. With a new confidence, he began to fumble around in the gloom, catching his hand against a switch on the wall, by the door, causing a single bare bulb, hanging loose on a flex in the ceiling, to fizz into a brightening glare. As his eyes adjusted to the sight, Woller was not much surprised to be looking at one room, one chair, one bed, one sink and one tap. One cupboard filled with cans of food, no bathroom and one spade. It was, however, quieter than elsewhere and warmer on the in than it was on the out, so, he shut the door, switched off the bare, fizzing bulb and fell on the bed in a sleeper of a heap. Woken again, with the sun, the soft light falling in odd shaped stripes as it came through the glass jars up on the window sill, it occurred to Woller that there was less than more to take his attention out in the marsh other than that which he had legged it out there to do, to get started in on the moodling. Then, quicker than a snap, he found himself sat up in the bed with a sudden realisation that he was not so much keen or convinced in his own mind about doing the moodling work that a moodler would do. This was not something he had thought long about when he first pinned down the notion of doing just that in the place he was in, though, now he was there, the prospect of becoming a moodler scared up something terrified. On first deciding to boot it over the fen to Skeldyke, with the intention of arranging his waking hours around the matter in hand, Woller had been keener than ever before, hoping that his engagement could be total and without interruption, allowing him to reach a rare sort of understanding. But then, he was caught in the brain with the realisation that he was, much sooner than he imagined he would be, less than more keen about doing anything of the sort. Worse than this, he was even less keen on the wooden shack, the blue painted door which was losing its peels and the leaning brick chimney that might lean to a fall, down through the rusting tin roof, crashing on top of whichever finker happened to be under it when it fell. If this were to happen, he reckoned it would not be a good thing. And the longer he thought about the where and the why of his own mattering means, sat in the shack, out in the nowhere of the middle of the marsh, thinking about finking and how to get it back, the more it became clear in his own mind that moodling was not for him. More than less sure, as he was, about this, however, Woller was not as easy in his relief about the decision as he thought he would be, when he realised that he had not been meeting the big talkers in the moodling tradition with whom it had been suggested he meet. But then, not a single one of the big talking moodlers had dropped him a word to wonder where he was, when he could have been elsewhere, leaving him to conclude that they had forgotten to remember, allowing him to remember to forget. This was a good thing as it gave him more of his own time, as much as he could want, to spend, back at the shack, under a blanket, beneath the rusting tin roof, curled up in the bed in a deep, gone sleeper. Only on the odd, thought leaking occasion, when he woke with one eye open, was he minded to ponder on that which he had hoped to have forgotten. Although, even then, he considered it to be not much more than his lack of other means to be meant or his own caring lack for these, when he could not move his loose hanging bones out of the bed, into his trousers, socks, jumper and shirt which were draped over the back of the chair. And when he could feel his brain on the sink, going down to a weight which took the rest of him with it, drumming out a slow rhythm on the inside of his own head as it did so, it occurred to him that it was a less than surprising new come reckoning that the what not, the when not and the how not to moodle, could be laid out at the feet of his own loose hanging bones. That they were hung as loose as they were was enough to bring on a wretched way of being, leaving only a husked and hollowed out shape of his own former self looking up at the underside of the rusting tin roof, unable to reach out through the blue peeler to the breeze. Laid flat on his back in the bed, he stared at nothing for what seemed a long lost while before closing his eyes, to make the staring stop, as he wondered what would happen to his mind and to his loose hung bones if he continued to do more of that than anything else. And then, sudden time quick, he chucked in the bed laid staring, when, leaping out and onto his feet, he tumbled out through the door of the shack, running off at a hurtling speed, over the marsh toward the sea. Skidding and lurching on his no boots feet, in his no trousers legs, his no shirt and no jumper arms, shoulders and chest, he went through and over the slurp, belching glop until he was brought to a slowing halt in the rough grass which grew long on the mud bank that sat as it was built, against the open weight of the Wash. Scrambling up the inner side and then stumbling down the outer side of the slope, clutching a pull at the grass with each of his hands as he did so, he tumbled himself down with a thump, hard and flat on the beach, just short of the water. Pulling himself up straight, he sat where he was and looked out, as his mind made off with the sea, leaving only his loose hanging bones sitting on the muddy sand in their tight skin wrapper, his mouth gaping open, as he tasted the salt on the wind. Then, as sudden as he had come, with a jumping shout, he was standing, caught hold by a judder of a teeth chattering shiver that sent his arms flailing at his sides and his feet stamping at the ground, as a shock of cold ran him through in a moment. Only now did Woller remember he was skinned bare, in the fen stark air which sent him flashing sharp, fleeting back over the bank and across the gloop to the small wooden shack, crashing through the peeling blue door, to fall into the bed and under the blanket that was still warm from before. Other than slowly bringing his shivering to a halt and warming his bones through, when he felt able to let his handed grip on the blanket slacken off, his hurling of his own mattering means back in the bed brought no sense of relief, no moment of grace from the pain in his brain. The aching and the tearing, the drumming and the drubbing which was constant and without pause, hammered in on him hard, causing him to reach out a hand, to feel about on the chair, at the side of the bed for his medicine needs. With the morfiner juice found and leaving a hand held around it tight, he pushed himself deeper into the snug of his bedding, reckoning on staying as he was until the pain loosened its hold. Whacked out and knackered as he lay where he was, juiced and fugged in his own mind, the realisation seeped in on his brain that wherever it was, it was not a good place for him to be and that he needed to get himself somewhere that was elsewhere, as soon as he could. As he pulled the blanket down from over his head, it was all he could do to stare out at the inside of the small wooden shack, at all that could be seen. The one room, the one chair, the one sink and the one tap. The one cupboard, now emptied of cans of food. And the one spade, leaning against the back wall where a bathroom might have been. It seemed to Woller, from where he was looking, laid on his side in the bed, with almost all of him under the blanket while still feeling the cold, to be colder and more spare than it could possibly be. He wondered where he could go from there. After a short time of head scratch, chin rubbing, he came to a decision, deciding that he would bag up and leg it home to Wisbech, back to his narrow, four storey town house with the three, deep grey, almost black, painted front doors. And so he did.

When he was not confused and tearing out his hair in a sudden come barker at the scrawling cracks, Woller was reading. And what he was reading, during the absence of confusion, tearing and barking moments, was a book which caused a crack of a sort, in his own mind. One which had not been there before. Whether it was seen as a bigger made line or a clearing out, it only came cracking through when he started to read the collected works of Doctor Mungo, who, he suggested, was without much doubt, one of the most important hum ha ponderers in the recent gone words of all hum ha pondering. At the same time, however, Woller also said that what he was doing came nowhere close to reading a hum ha ponderers words, claiming, as he did that he could never be interested in the opinions of a hum ha ponderer who actively considered himself to be such a thing. What was hum ha pondering anyway? Define it, he challenged his friends and those who knew him, even though it seemed that none of them could. A definition of such a thing appeared to be easier said than had. As a consequence of this, it was thought about and it was talked about, it was scrawled about and it was drawn about, to the point where it seemed to become only more confused in the minds of those finkers who were doing the talking, the scrawling and the drawing. Caught, as each and all of them were, in a welter of their own making, there were some who thought it would be over and done when none of the finkers who were doing the talking, the scrawling and the drawing could remember what it was that had been thought at the time. The finkers in question scratched their heads and blinked their eyes until each and all of them shrugged up, then shrugged down, a shoulder in turn, before wandering off, each with their own thoughts, to wherever a quiet corner could be found. Woller was not quite such a keener for their sort of forgetting. What he *was* keen on was the long scrawled work that Doctor Mungo had completed on the smiling of a smile and the reasoning fink for taking a benign wander through the meaning of each gone day. To know how he could do this, as well as asking why he would want to, was just what he *was* keening for. And on the occasions when he was less than able to do so, he wanted to know why it was he could *then* not. Woller reckoned that even though he had been seduced in his own mind by the words of a wandering peddler, such a reaction was reasonable enough when a count of those other finkers who had also been seen to hang on the words of Doctor Mungo, was taken into consideration. These were thought to be worth reading for any finker with ideas to be had, though, as some had said, the thinking of them and the scrawling of them were as much a confirmation of a wider finking approach as a handing down and out of dog eared sentiment. And it seemed to Woller that on discovering for himself the collected works of Doctor Mungo, he had taken a whack, of a bracing sort, to clear his mind, earlier than might otherwise have been the case. All were agreed it was a curious thing that smiling had proved to be such a catcher for the hum ha pondering of Doctor Mungo, who, insisted it was the principal factor with regard to the mattering means, causing him to come down hard on what he saw as a fastening hold on learning ideals. In particular, those that explained how accepted thoughts which were handed out and down, were ones to be had. With his own research he suggested that because it was instinctive, a smile could not be given out, taken away or wiped clean. A smile was the one and only thing it could be. This was a profound contention, encouraging, as it did, a curious scratching of heads and rubbing of chins, about the how, the what and the when of an objective fact; something which some thought to be a questionable notion as it was. A question that was asked by the finkers and the fennermarsh people too, was, if Doctor Mungo could claim to have discovered the existence of a single trait, how had he reached such a conclusion? Throughout the wider finking community, a long floor paced debate had raged as to exactly how the skin, bone and sack filled gloop could come to be hung up, pegged out or otherwise, with the head forcing the shrinkers and the twisters of the inner, to the outer of the mattering means. The formerly filled versus the filling required argument remained less than little disputed than it had been for earlier gone generations of finkers. Other questions to be asked were, how had Doctor Mungo come to determine what could affect the stand, the sit, the spit, the fidget and the fumble, the look, the touch and the stumble of the skin that fixed a wrapper on the means which mattered (or if not, then at least the other way around) or were the loose hung bones more of one thing than another? And were the means for the smiler a manifestation of something deep down on the inside, not to be reasoned with a piece of a marrow? Hum ha, thought each and all of those who were asking the questions and hoping for answers, even though there were also some who were aware that there would be none to be had, as Doctor Mungo was interested in being questioned only when he decided he wanted to be. What he *was* interested in, other than boozers, beds and joy faking hookers, was searching for whatever could be thought to be new. And the what of his search that was newer than not was a smile. One which was sometimes to be seen while at other times might be gone or not ever been, depending on the where and the when of those of a squealing sort, with their understanding of right and wrong. There was much that Doctor Mungo was wanting to know because he thought the smile and the smiler could be found wherever the fennermarsh people were, in the fens of the east and the west and the south and the north, smiling a smile to be seen as amused, bemused, tight, bright, winning, grinning, wry, ironic and even iconic. There were, however, those of a censorious sort who were not much pleased about such own knowing means being given out wide, with no concern for the consequences. And not least that which each and all of them considered to be wrong rather than right. As a result, there were some who were thought to be smiling for the wrong reasons which were leaking through to a vulnerable mind, eventually coming down with a triggered snap from someone or other in a bone cracking mood of a frowning grump. With a flawed understanding of the situation, Doctor Mungo was of the opinion that there was nothing to be done, so nothing was what he did, other than to furrow his brow in response. That such furrowing was not the end of the matter as he might have thought was obvious enough, when he was talking, told about how his bothering lack could be seen as a suggestion of his being more often wrong than was good for him. With a sudden lurch in his brain, he caught a sense of what it would mean to be encouraged in a better way of thinking, moving him to give it as much of a clearing steer as he could. As far as Woller was concerned, there was no reason even for the flicker of a lash, especially when he thought he understood more about Doctor Mungo than less or recognised at least, a way of being, a raring to be haring, with a keening wont, for a must have piece of own made space in a looping shape. And then, there was their sharing a need to walk everywhere and anywhere, a continual booting up and legging it out, in the rain, the snow, the heat and the cold. Walking for miles through the streets, over the bridges spanning the rivers, along the sides of the wide cut drains, under the trees which stood at the sides of the running creeks and on to the sea, whether the sun was up high or down low in the sky and fat to be seen, orange over the flat land.

At the end of a slow morning in the last week of the month, as he sat almost on his own in a quiet dinner shop, Woller was caught in the brain with the realisation that he could be any other where but where he was. In spite of the fact that he had been back home for only a brief flash of recent time, his fascination with the place was turning into a choking that he needed to get out and let loose before he set his own means down as thoroughly miserable and all scratched out. And so he got up from being sat to go through and out of the door of the dinner shop into the street, to make a telephone call to Virginia Wane – Zane. A shortened hour later, as Woller was making his own boot legged way out of town, he slowly became aware that Tabitha Greeling was close beside him keeping the same pace as his boots, all the while looking at him in a curious way. That she had not spoken a word and seemed to be pleased just to be walking was something he thought was either odder than odd or less than more odd than it might have been, knowing, as he did, who it was. Woller reasoned that she might have decided to take a walk, when, then without much realising it, she found herself on the road next to him. And not knowing what to do, she had done nothing but continue in a sort of surprised, somewhat bemused manner. On the other hand, she could have purposely come up alongside his own rolling stride in order to talking, tell him whatever it was that had been on her mind since the last time the two of them had seen each and the other. But Tabitha Greeling had not made a sound, other than the noise of her shoes, as they clacked on the road as she walked. The two of them, the one next to the other, booted and shoed their same going way until they reached the edge of Wisbech, where Woller came to a sudden quick stop. Tabitha Greeling stopped a pace further on and turned around and looked, not at him but at a button which was hanging loose on a length of pale blue thread, three quarters of the way up the

front of her long summer coat. Seeing that she was about to
fiddle and faff with it, something, he reckoned which would
distract them both, her and him, Woller asked her to leave the
loosened button where it was. She forewent what she had been
about to do, looked at him and for the first time that morning,
spoke a word or more. She had only wanted to say hello, she
said but not being too sure of how to say such a simple thing
she had said nothing at all, continuing instead, to walk without
speaking, embarrassed that she had not done the first and could
not stop doing the other. She said this and then closed her eyes,
standing where she was without moving as though not seeing.
And not being seen, either by Woller or anyone else. Looking
back at Tabitha Greeling as she stood, it came on sharp to
Woller that he was caught in the throat with the moment as it
was. Caught out with his own forgetting. And even though he
knew there were words he could say, to the standing girl, with
the loosening thread, he could not think quite how to say them.
So he did not. All he could think to tell her, in the only talking
words he could then find, was that he needed to be gone, to
clear his own mind and boots out of town, to be free and
thinking on his feet as they took him over to the western fen.
He could not talk with another finking talker when he was
pared down to a nervous and whacked out sack of bones such
as he was, he said. Tabitha Greeling saw less than much point in
arguing and so let him go without hurling any words of her
own, standing where she was, as she had been but now with the
pricking of tears in her reddening eyes. She watched him as he
moved further away, walking by and under the plane trees that
were lined straight on either side of the road, as the crows from
the nests, in the tops of those trees, wheeled and cawed, high
above in the air. She watched him until, eventually, he merged
with the fields way off in the distance and was gone from sight.
As he walked, it occurred to Woller that he was now less than

more sure about exactly why he had said the words he had to Tabitha Greeling, finding it hard to decide if he had meant to say them or not. All he knew was that he had said them and that she had listened to him saying them. And that she had looked back at him with a look of quiet bewilderment, not speaking again after that moment. When he realised that he could not continue looking at her without doing something he might later wish that he hadn't, he left on a heel, causing her she and his he, each and the other, to be alone there in the fen. And this was sooner and not later than the earlier keening with which he had been filled. One of packing, bagging and legging it off in his boots, to spend more than enough of both time and cash in whichever hooking house he could get himself in through the door of first. Accordingly, he tried to remember the first time he had found himself knocked against a cash taking, joy faking hooker, though, he was not much trusting of his own remembering. With a vague memory, he thought that the first time knocking could have been a long time before when he had come to know Virginia Wane – Zane who could make available, sooner than most, the charms of a peach arsed woman. Aware of the sale of a clambering feel, those who came to Wigtoft fen were given over to an easy opinion of the hooking women and their various places of fumbled work. And for those who were there, to sell what they could, a sleight of hand fumble was offered as a promise of a good time for anyone cashed up enough to come through the doors in a keening rush. As there were no secrets or moralising notions, crammed in oddly matched socks, the cash taking was a continual raking in for the joy making fakers, each of whom was a model for a crisp egalitarianism, taking cash from anyone and everyone, with special consideration only for those who were broke. And cash was given by whom so ever had it to give, as well as from some with less than most to spare, though, still wanting to be done at the discretion of some of the fakers, at some of the places. With a well worn nod to passing trade, there were hooking houses in Wigtoft fen that were as much of a part of the local boozers as the stools, the pumps and the booze at the bar. The joining together of commercial interests was an obvious, sense making thing when the boozers were jammed to bursting with guzzling thirsters. And where the cash taking, joy faking sort, could weave their almost dressed selves, for rent, through the crowds of yelling men with sweating necks, grabbing hands and goggling eyes. As obvious too, was that the boozers, the thirsters and the almost dressed, joy faking hookers, could be a combustible combination, leading, on occasion to moments of smack whacking violence, though, not so bad and only on occasion. More often than not, such places were quiet, attracting the sort of melancholic, alcoholic stool huncher, who simply wanted to sink down, heavy and alone at the bar, with their fingers clasped around a glass of booze. It occurred to Woller that although the western fen was the place in which he had first been sparked in his brain with the fleeting charms of the fakers of joy, there had been other times after that and in other places when he had thought about taking his bones to hooking houses, where smiling women were taking cash from damp pocketed men. And he had thought about doing so in the company of Thelonius Greeling, a man with a missus to his mister, to know about and object to the happening of it, in the event she would have been told. As he walked and thought about what he had been thinking then, in contrast to the thoughts he was thinking now, he was caught with the realisation that his boots had begun to slow from a stride, to a stroll, to an amble and then to a shuffle. It seemed that whatever it was he could be thinking now, it was not the same as whatever it might have been before. Stranger still, he was less than more keen to arrive than he had been when he had first started out, as he stopped his boots with the shuffling and stood where he was. On looking down at them both with a reasoning lack, he was confused about why he had been as keen, as he had, to leave Tabitha Greeling behind in the road. After a while of standing, as the time turned slower and began to kick itself in the heels, he recognised, could see easily enough that he did not know why he had. And that was that. What he *did* know was that his reckoning was off its kilter and in need of some care, so, rather than keeping on with the loosening pull of the western fen hookers, he decided that this was the moment to clear off back, in the direction from which he had come. Such a decision, however, took him by surprise in his turning mind, with a turn on his boots too. And with no hint of a warning, he found himself falling in a clatter, down in a ditch. There he remained, in a heap of his loose hanging bones, doing nothing but thinking, staring and despairing, at his sudden come, falling lapse, to a quick handed tearing at his own hair. As he sort of sat and sort of lay, heaped at sharp angles, at the bottom of the ditch, among the reeds and the coarse grass, the smell of the wet earth filling his nostrils, it seemed to Woller that he ought to make some sort of a move. Although, he was less than more sure about why he ought to or even how he could do so, when he did not know where it was that he wanted to move to. And bigger than this, he reckoned he ought to do something to make a difference, wider than his immediate need to reach a conclusion and get pinning it down, even as it began to seep into his fuzzing brain that the only thing he *was* clear about was his reluctance to decide on much of anything at all. The urgency was gone as he sank his own means, back, amongst the reeds and the coarse grass at the bottom of the ditch, flattened out in a calm hanging of time, quick spent, with seemingly nowhere to go and nothing else to do, other than to ponder on the absurd turn of events. All of which seemed reasonable enough for a finker to do, though, he was also caught with the realisation that there was a knowing lack in his mind which was more in need of the meedler vong than ever before. The meedler vong, however, had no ideals, no mattering means, no friends, no roots and no boots, leaving Woller made better aware that even though he might well have needed the meedler vong, it had no need of him.

Wollers return to Wisbech coincided with a crisis in the family
of Thelonius Greeling. Such a thing in itself was less than more
of a surprise to their friends and those who knew them, as the
mister to the missus, the daughter and the son had for a long
time gone been teetering on a wobble, just waiting for
something to crash down on their heads. The one head in
particular which had suddenly cracked was that of Tabitha
Greeling. If there had been any cracks in the bone through to
the brain earlier than then, these had now widened out and
broken open, exposing her minded thoughts and her talking
words to small reason. And though he was struck with a harder
than usual sense that he had no personal urging to be pulled
along with this flailing girl, Woller, was, nonetheless, caught in
the throat with the feeling that he ought to turn himself up at
such a catastrophic breach on the inside of the red brick town
house on the river Nene. And so he did. He arrived at the
outside of the white painted front door at the same moment as
the medicine man, who, on being called out by Cordelia
Greeling, also arrived with his knuckles raised for a knock. As
Woller had already knocked with a knuckled hand, Cordelia
Greeling opened the door from the inside before either could
speak to the other and quicker than sharp, she ushered them
through to the hall. And down to the kitchen where Tabitha
Greeling was curled in a ball, on the table, in the middle of the
room. The medicine man sat down on a chair and looked at his
patient. He looked at her with his head cocked to the left. And
he looked at her with his head cocked to the right. He leaned
towards her for a closer look. And then he leaned back for a
better look at all of her bones. He poked her between the ribs
with one of his fingers. He prodded each of her thighs with a
pencil. And then he rubbed his chin, scratched his head and
sucked at his teeth before letting out a low whistle. Eventually,
he opened his bag and absent mindedly thumbed a corner of

the licensing card he had only recent time been given. A card which allowed him to make a diagnosis, suggest a prognosis and even to hand out a neurosis. Tabitha Greeling looked at the medicine man and he looked back at her. But still, he sat on the chair and said nothing. Then, in a sudden rush and with no hint of a warning, he stood up in his shoes and straight out diagnosed a fever of sorts, speaking his words as quick as he could before clutching tight a hold on his bag and hurtling off at a run, out of the kitchen, down the hall, through the front door and outside to the street and away. Those in the kitchen who were stood looking at the patient girl curled on the table, were left wondering whether or not to take the hurriedly dispensed opinion of the medicine man seriously, though, even to consider such a thing seemed to be anything but sensible. So none of them did. Instead, they settled on the notion that although the fever of sorts might well have grabbed a hold on Tabitha Greelings brain and thrown her off from the small patch of clarity to which she had been clinging, it was in all probability not the only cause of her sudden quick decline. She had continually said to her friends and those who knew her that she felt cracked to the point where to take another blow would see her crack wide open, beyond repair. Worse still, she had been scared up something terrified that one of them would decide to help her in a way that she would not want to be helped. And so, Tabitha Greeling had wailed and screeched to be spared the curious prodding's of the mind stealing couch hoppers and their dog eared concern, their banal hum ha analysis of her various disappointments, her constant frustrations and her numerous betrayals. She begged to be spared their lack of understanding. In the maternal mind of Cordelia Greeling it was clear enough that though such things could have been contributing factors in her daughters loosening hold on reality and ought, therefore, not be dismissed, the obvious cause of her arm wrapped, knee clutched table curling, was seated deep in a quite particular sack of loose hanging bones. Cordelia Greeling did not say the words out loud, she only looked hard at Woller. Having earlier decided that it would better for him if he appeared to know less than most about events as they were, Woller smiled back at Cordelia Greeling in the face of her hardening look. Cordelia Greeling looked away and wondered instead what could be done for her curling girl. All she could know was that a diagnosis of a fever of sorts was worth less than she hoped, with the explanation given being cast in a vague direction from a general position rather than specifically administered with care and concern. The most that could be said was that it was what it was. It had been noticed and noted then passed down the line for someone else to deal with. And so it was. Tabitha Greeling was funnelled through a system of forms and files, serious thoughts and urgent talk that told of nothing more than the name and number of the girl at the end of its reach, lying small and curled on the table in the kitchen from where she refused to be moved. It occurred to her, as she lay where she did, on top of the table at which she had often sat to drink with her father or to eat with her mother, to talk and to shout, both with and at all of them together, how the funnelling of forms and the furrowing of brows above hard rubbed chins would make less than much of a difference to the condition she was in. With this in mind, she thought there seemed to be small point in staying where she was, waiting for a labelling of her own brain on a form at the communal hospital before fading away in a bed on a ward at the end of a corridor, with a reasoning lack. And no hope of a helping hand. So she got down from the table and hauled her cracked sack of bones away as the assembled lookers, each and all of them, stopped with their talking to stare in silence when she began to move in a slow, wobbling way, out of the kitchen, down through the hall and on up the stairs to her room. Woller went too, quick footing it through the hall, out of the front door and down the steps to the street which he hit in his shoes at a run, making a minded note as he did so, to not go back for as long as it took for Tabitha Greeling to be sparkling clean and smiling again. Cordelia Greeling was relieved to see the table free but she was, nonetheless, concerned about her daughters unusual behaviour over how and what was to be done on the question of her keeping going without curling in a ball whenever she could. Thelonius Greeling said that he too was just as concerned for her sudden cracked mind but he was even less of a whistler than the medicine man on the question of how it could be brought to a resolving end. He sat himself down on a chair to think. At the end of a long while of scratching his head and staring at Cordelia Greeling, as she stared back at him, he announced that he had found a solution to the problem of what was to be done. The solution was to be found in the form of Walter Wotsisname, he said. Thelonius Greeling had been only short time and vaguely acquainted with the young man known to most as Walter Wotsisname. All of which caused Cordelia Greeling some alarm. And even on the few occasions when the two of them had met, neither of them had said enough to encourage the one to want to know more about the other. This did not, however, seem to be a stopper of a point for Thelonius Greeling as without so much of a talk with the missus to his mister, he telephoned Walter Wotsisname to arrange a booze drinking afternoon of spoken words on the matter of Tabitha Greeling. It seemed that Walter Wotsisname was stretched to bursting with his own curious need to know the reason why he had been asked for a boozing drink, with someone he hardly knew, when he turned himself up, clammer bang hammering his knuckles on the outside of the white painted front door of the red brick town house, on the river

Nene. Cordelia Greeling opened the door from the inside and showed him through to the sitting room where the mister to her missus was sat, in his favourite armchair in front of the open hearth. When, at a time that was later and not sooner after he had earlier arrived, Walter Wotsisname had drunk down too much of the booze which Thelonius Greeling had been pouring with abandon into the glasses that each of them clutched in their hands, he could not even recall why it was he was there or where exactly *there* was. It was at this moment of forgetting that Thelonius Greeling saw an opportunity. And so, with all reason soaked away with the booze, not to mention the promise of a cash filled account, Walter Wotsisname was persuaded to softly, nicely and maybe not so wisely, ask Tabitha Greeling to hitch up with him and become a new made missus, as given to his mister. On being helped up to her room by his mother and father in law to come, his wobbling legs would not carry him further than the top of the stairs, crumpling him into a heap, half on the landing, coughing his way through a chuckle at what he was doing. Gathering his thoughts, he smiled at Cordelia Greeling but she only poked a finger into his ribs and jerked her head to one side, in the direction of her daughter. Walter Wotsisname took his cue and bellowed out his proposal across the landing. Sitting alone on the floor in her room, staring at her feet, Tabitha Greeling was scared up something terrified when she heard the bellowing of the proposing Walter Wotsisname on the other side of her door, coming, as it did, in such a sudden rush. Odder still, she then caught her own self with surprise when the answer she gave was a yes, as she stood up, quick on her feet and shouted it loud through the door. And then she sat down again on the floor, to stare at her hands. Out on the landing, Walter Wotsisname smiled to himself then passed out where he sat, in a booze filled sleeper. Thelonius and Cordelia Greeling, each and the other, were no less surprised than their own daughter at her sudden response to the hitching question, especially when there seemed to be a measure of calm in her voice as she assured the two of them that even though she had not done much of the choosing, she saw no point in the matter being any way other than the way that it was. She would be happy to go, she said. On hearing this, both her mother and her father were struck with relief at the thought of the girl being better off, away from the kitchen of their red brick town house. A trigger as large as the family table might serve only to remind her of what it was to fall, either there or elsewhere, lost in a field or out in the street, sat, down on the ground in a crease of her own making. When Woller was talking told by Thelonius Greeling from the other end of a telephone line about the recent time events on his stairs, he knew, in his own mind, could feel in his bones, a sense of relief. The weight of whatever it had been, the feeling of being, in some way, responsible, for the hurtled decline in the behaviour of Tabitha Greeling, seemed to have lifted, he thought. This, he reckoned, was a good thing, not least because he had been less than more keen on taking a glare from Cordelia Greeling on the seemingly delicate matter of her daughters emotional mind. And now that he was no longer held to account for the actions of a girl who could draw her own means into a curling shape, he found he could breathe, once again, with an ease which he thought he had earlier lost. As Woller thought about the way things were at the red brick town house, on the river Nene, he wondered whether his being there on the warmer side of the white painted front door would make matters better or worse. After a hum ha moment, the answer was obvious enough. And with that he took a clearing steer, as wide as he could.

Some time toward the end of August, it occurred to Woller that he needed to start on the foot bashing, door banging, mind slogging work which he knew he had to be doing now that he was out for a kilter from the well worn and the familiar. The better dressed brother of the curious Amos Cloot was the first person he decided to approach. As a former collectivist of note come connector to most, he had succeeded, with the encouragement of some, in becoming known to the finkers in the cultural elites of Gosberton Clough and Tydd Gote. The well dressed brother, was, therefore, a man of some regard. In addition, he was also the founding editor of a curious journal that he had, for a longer time than he could remember, cashed up and controlled. And though he had no close finker connections of his own, he was, for some reason or other, looked on as a zinger of a contact for finking creative brains with his connecting number continually being passed on, by those who passed through, even when his cracked record was anything but good. And so, apart from an initial hurling of encouraging words, the well dressed brother of Amos Cloot did nothing at all. On hearing about this, Oscar Sollermon offered to write a letter of introduction to pink cheeked Polly who then ran a boodler press in collaboration with a long time friend. One who was enthusiastic about less than much other than boozing. A man, who claimed to be on speaking terms with the meedler vong. A claim that was, in the main, dismissed. Woller, was, nevertheless, keener than most and soon time quick he turned himself up on the outside of the scratched front door of the large, pale yellow house on Gull Bank that was home to pink cheeked Polly and her booze soused companion. Standing where he was on a chipped stone path, he gave the door a knuckling bang. In the top left pocket of his coat, there was a letter addressed to pink cheeked Polly in his own handed scrawl which was supposed to explain the reason for his scrawling it. Also, he was hoping to give her a large brown paper envelope inside of which were several typed pages of the opening chapters of a manuscript to serve as examples of his own finking work, along with the letter of introduction from Oscar Sollermon. In the event, the door of the house was opened by a white haired woman of long gone years, who, evidently, was not pink cheeked Polly but someone else entirely. The white haired woman looked at Woller for a moment before taking the letter of introduction, along with the large brown paper envelope, out of his hands, while, at the same time, telling him that she was the only person in the house and would be for another thirteen and a quarter days. Woller, was, on hearing these words, down in a grump on his worn through soles. The white haired woman of well gone years, assured him, however, in a sharp sounding tone that pink cheeked Polly would respond to his door stepped delivery as soon as she was back on the inside of the house. In spite of her manner, it seemed to Woller there was nothing more that could have been said, so he took a swallow of sorts and went home to his four storey town house, with the three, deep grey, almost black, painted front doors, walking on a quieter heel than he might otherwise have done. Thirteen and a quarter days later, the large brown paper envelope containing the typed manuscript pages, along with the letter of introduction from Oscar Sollermon, came crisp, crackling through his door with a shorter than anticipated note of gloom. Ha hum, said Woller, amongst other things. As he wondered what could be done, it occurred to him that with a number of their own no fewer than those who thought of themselves as publishers, there were commissioning editors to be asked *for* and begged *from* by a desperate finker looking for work. There was an occasional rumour about one editor or another who could be persuaded to take on a free associating finker worth a scrawling go, on a journal or a cheap sold squealer. One commissioning editor after another was nothing if not courteous with their speaking words, though, no less dismissive, as each and all of them refused to offer even the vaguest promise of cash paid work. Woller thought the courtesy, at least, was a good thing. And so, whacked, cracked and hammered hard down with disappointment, he did what seemed the only thing to be done as he dropped his loosening sack of bones into bed and fell into a sleeper.

In a vague sort of way, Woller had become aware that there was a peculiar feel to his own known means. There appeared to be a change to the matter of each day, even though it was something he could only sense and not quite pin down which slipped on through the length, the depth and the breadth of his entire boned, blood filled sack of a being. Worse than this, he was also without knowing what it meant, what he was supposed to think about it and more urgently, what he was supposed to do. Was he supposed to do anything at all? Hum ha, hum ha, he thought, as he ran a hand through his hair until it was stood straight up on end. As much as he needed to, he found the clearing of his mind harder to do than some would have thought. And even though he gave it as long as he could, there was not much more than a scratch of frustration and wailed annoyance. With a long belled sound, the telephone rang. On picking up the receiver, he heard the voice of Agnes Mortimer coming through in a rush of spoken words, telling him things he was less than more sure he wanted to hear. What he could gather from the worded sounds rushing in his ear was news of a creeping authoritarianism which could soon enough be seen in the form of a suggested censorship of publications act. Woller was much concerned to be told about this when it had slipped through and by him, even though it had been seen by Agnes Mortimer along with the finkers of the cultural elites of Gosberton Clough and Tydd Gote. Indeed, each and all of them had said words of their own which were then wider discussed on the pressing necessity of understanding the meaning of such a suggestion, in order to make a concerted effort to oppose it. Talking about doing was not however, *doing* in itself and as a consequence, nothing was done to challenge those dog eared creepers who were keen on the suggesting of rules. Although there were some of a finking sort who thought that a censorship of publications act was a strange one to be proposed, by those with no direct influence on events, there were others who saw that the notion of influence was a curious thing, being controlled by no none but given over to a long enough reach. Wherever it came from, a resulting act would be designed to provide for the censoring of those works whose general tendency ran counter to any and all doctrines which some wanted to be introduced so that everyone could recognise a right way to be done and a wrong way to be gone, with no manoeuvring room for confusion. Such was the exactitude of the ideal that if ever the suggested new act was folded out and put into play, it could be no small coincidence that there would turn out to be an extraordinarily high volume of such counter run works. A quiet spoken promise was made that the censuring of the wrong scrawlers and of the wrong scrawled books could be organised with a remarkable turn of speed. And though none of the fennermarsh people knew much about the how or the what of that which was happening around them with a sleighted hand, they were, nonetheless, slow blinked aware of loosening a hold on something of value, of a sounded call, with a loss that would only be felt when a familiar voice was gone. As a consequence, there were chattered rumours in the boozers and on the streets, on the matter of thinking about the meedler vong. And what was said, by those who were concerned more than most, was that sooner and not later the meedler vong would fall out of favour too.

Woller was much concerned with his own there and then, in particular, with a publisher in Boston who had promised him an answer about Colonel Haw and the Clatterball within weeks of his first taking in the manuscript. That however, had been then. And now, when he was rattling in his bones with a fast losing measure of patience, the earlier promise seemed to be of less than more worth than he had thought, leaving him with a reckoning that he was almost where he did not want to be. Understanding well enough where he was, he knew that an acceptance of Colonel Haw and the Clatterball would completely change his own less than much appreciated circumstances, giving him the means, to ease, into a sufficiently cashed condition to keep him alive. And more importantly, to leave him with a reason to keep on keeping on as a live finker without the constant need to wonder about the how of a sudden shot bang to the brain. Odd as he thought and strange as he did, he strung himself out with the clock, in a foot paced, floor stretched loop of the attic of his four storey town house with the three, deep grey, almost black, painted front doors, rubbing at his chin as he went. And as he waited too. The waiting he hated, more than he could say. When his ears began to hiss with the heat he could feel leaking out from inside his brain, he called Oscar Sollermon on the telephone in order to talk and to yell, as he coughed, retched and clung on with exhausted nerves as he haw hawed at the appearance of his own self, reflected, in the glass of the small window at which he was stood. He asked Oscar Sollermon for a way of knowing the answer to his question of how it was possible to be so far down in the manner of a desperate keener that a finker could not even care what was said to and about them, as they listened to the words which were talked out loud in their direction by a trampler of long held dreams. Talked at, by someone who might decide *to* or might decide *not to* publish his poured out finking work. But even though he had been asked, Oscar Sollermon could not think how he could help as he knew no more than Woller did himself. Woller put down the telephone and continued his route with the slow rounded, ground out time of the long leg pacing. The weeks and the patience fell away. And with all that too, more head ripped hair appeared loose stranded in his hands when Woller decided to scrawl a note to the publisher in Boston asking if a decision on Colonel Haw and the Clatterball had been made. No answer came. The lack of words good or bad bashed him in hard so that he sat back and down in a slump, as all ambition began to fall inward, collapsing around him in a crumple, folding itself into nothing. The essence of the matter for his own known needs, was that more than most, the scrawling words were a breathing, feeding and reasoning line of sanity which gave him a sense of finking regard. A sense to be remembered by a finker who had fallen down a hole, such as he had. And even though he knew well enough just how caught he was in the narrowing trim of it all, there was, in his mind, a refusal to accept the blurring of once sharp edges which were now and then fogged as if his finking were beginning to wear out and slow. Something was causing him to lean against the words and the sounds of those around him in order to understand his own mattering means. This much was obvious enough. And he had no idea how to survive intact, aware as he was that both the wearing and the slowing could be a keeler of a crushing blow to his continuing means to matter. Understanding his own need to make even the smallest move of a recovering sort, Woller deciding on a walking cure. And doing so with a legged foot, boot slogged, wandering gait without pause, he could and he did walk in his boots to the clapped out verge of exhaustion, through the streets, beside the rivers and along the tops of the watered cuts, over the fields and across the fen to the edge of the mud where the marsh oozed into the sea. If the timing was good and the weather set fair, the skies cracked through with a brightening light, he would make a final check to see if his head was set firm on his neck. Then he would drop out and slip down, from the inside to the outside, into a minded state which cut him loose from the muffled foot stomping and his own ground hogging tether. There were other times too, when the tethering sense that he hoped to escape held more than less of a pull than he imagined it would, pulling him to the flat without even a warning shout. This was not a good thing, he knew that. It would be, he thought, at such a sudden come moment as slipping and sliding his way through a wet grassed field that he might be caught with enough of a start to urge him to pick up his boots in a run, stumbling out through a gate and into a lane. And even though he could see the reasoning lack as he was moved to think noo wah and then noo wah again, it was a surprising thing to Woller that he could not easily shake from his mind the possible fright of his own legged flight from a deserted field. In coping with this, he was reckoned on guessing the weight of a feeling when the shape of it was lost to his own knowing mind, more than before. When he then thought it over, it occurred to him that it might be a teller of a sign that his present hanging around, kicking up his heels, was set on a running a course that he well knew, so familiar did it seem. Although, coming to a realisation of whatever sort, was not something he was able to use. And even if it was, he had been, earlier than then, less than more sure about how much of a change in his circumstances could be wrought, regardless of the action he might take. With his bones hanging as loose as they were, he was caught hard to wonder if he could haul himself up from wherever it was he had sunk to get his feet on their own balance again. Added to this, he could not or at least he *would* not speak to his friends and those who knew him about the worsening turn he was taking or about what had been *the almost always reliable* sign of a gathering crisis. On the morning of the seventeenth day in August, Oscar Sollermon pitched himself up on the outside of the four storey town house with the three, deep grey, almost black, painted front doors and gave the one in the middle a bang of a knuckle. As the door opened, he saw Woller, standing on the inside with a creased expression fading from his face in recognition of the outside knuckler. Oscar Sollermon held up a hand to stop him from speaking before he could start. Woller said nothing. And he did almost the same, except to allow a half smile to push at the corners of his mouth, as he looked back at Oscar Sollermon stood in the street in front of his house, holding up his left hand in a silencing gesture. Although he was there at the door, Oscar Sollermon said, in as many words as he could but in fewer than he might that he would not be a stayer on, only a dropper in. And then, a short time hurrier off again. What he was not intending to do was take off his shoes and hang around for longer than the time it would take because he was in something of a rush to hop to it, in an effort to move his own bones as far as Donington in the western fen before it was too late to do so. Woller did not ask why this was. While Oscar Sollermon did not say, other than to explain that he had only taken the risk to call in on Woller so he could see with his own two eyes that his fellow finking friend *was,* from his head on his neck, to his feet in his shoes, *still where he was,* where he had *been,* earlier than then. As alive as he could hope him to be. Oscar Sollermon said that he could see very well without the need for much more than a quick sharp look that Woller was indeed still as alive as he had been before. And then he left, leaving behind him the hollow of a middle of nowhere feeling which scared up Woller something terrified, enough that he found a quickening pace in his own feet which ran in his shoes at a sole doubled lick. When Oscar Sollermon had gone, Woller stepped outside from behind his door number two, sat his loose hanging bones down in a slump, in the street and tried to remember how things *had* been, before they were now. In what he thought of as a vain attempt, he tried to haul from his memory a recall of the days, the weeks and the months he had spent with his own, what he knew of it, self in Wisbech. He thought about the girl from Terrington St. Clement. And he thought about Agnes Mortimer. He thought about not thinking about Clementine Murnegan. And he thought he ought not to have forgotten how Catherine Cole had looked. It was then, with a soon come catch in his throat that he realised his old gone thinking was not a good thing as it seemed only to remind him of the peculiar, solitary situation into which he had fallen. The thought of taking root and sticking fast in a particular place was enough to shake his bones through to their softening core, beginning, as he was, to feel a sliding desperation to see those friends whom he had not so much left behind but left out and gone. All of which caused him to be worried as to whether or not this need of his to see them would be reciprocated. As a result of his veering off and losing balance over something that had louder than before, banged around in his brain and tugged at his sleeve as a new thing, old thing, his needing to bawl became more pressing, the longer he was where he was. In spite of this and his vague hum ha wondering about the where of most of his friends and those who knew him, he was aware that he seemed to have put up his feet on the circumstances as they were, not least on those of Clementine Murnegan. What he had not known, as he had not asked, so had not been told, was that Clementine Murnegan was laid in a bed in the communal hospital in a fading curl, conked out for the count and losing fast to a knackered, broken down sack of bones. One which could no longer maintain a hold on her own mattering means. And no more could she kick hard in a shortened scuffle, wracked as she was with hurt lurches and hoarse croaked words. With a heaving loss of her breathing before a leaving off from where she had started, Clementine Murnegan was dead. That she was no longer a breather or a gasper or even a starer out of her ranging eyes which had been sat, hollow deep, in her thinned face, was a surprise to those who had been with her when she went, as the medicine man who had been there for the tending of her bones had talking told them that she was almost, nearly to the end, mended. The discharging department at the communal hospital then announced that if the medicine man who had been sent to attend to Clementine Murnegans sack of old bones was holding on to his medical opinion that the patient in question was well enough to be discharged, then his opinion would be implemented, quick time sharp. Quicker still if she were found to be dead. On hearing of the death of Clementine Murnegan, it struck Woller that he could simply have imagined it so much less than real did it seem. And even if it *had* been an actual happened event, he could not recall who it was who had told him, other than a flicker of a moment of someone doing the telling, as he listened, with not quite believing ears, whenever and wherever he had been at the time that he was. What concerned him more than otherwise was his forgetting to remember the how of it being done. And the feel of the rolling over within his own brain at the time that he heard the sounded voice of the teller, though, barely understanding the meaning in jagged stops. He was minded to think he was quick to care when the how of it was gone. Sooner and not later all he had left was an aching need in his own self to leave, to get off and get legged away, to be somewhere that was elsewhere and not where he was. And though he was reeling on his feet with his balance having taken a doubting whack, he realised that he what he needed to do was more than simply move. There was action to be taken in a big decision manner, to change for the better the going of wherever he was slow crawl and without direction heading. The immediate and only solution that sat him up with a starting bang was to head out across the fen to Crowland. And so he did.

Woller turned himself up in the town early on the morning of the twenty ninth day of September, as the bells in the high tower of the abbey were ringing out the time. Without knowing why, he tried out a quick pretence in his brain of a belled ring just for him as a welcoming sound. Then quicker again, he was caught with the thought that such a thing could be scarce wanted causing him to change his mind over to something else instead; to whatever would be less than more of a concern. As he walked to the end of a street and came to a stop where it joined with the ends or the beginnings he could not see which well enough, of two other streets, he found himself stood on a corner, looking, at what he reckoned was the most curious stone bridge he had ever seen. With a blinked count of its sides he could see there were three, each with steps for walking a wandering crosser from each of the different ways to a point at the top in the middle, from where a crossing wanderer could either stand and stare out at the town or get back down to the ground at one of the three streets with a beginning or an end. With a bringer of a dizzying scratch to a confounded head, there seemed to be an obvious absence of water in a flow under the bridge. And no matter in which direction Woller took a squint against the brightening sun, he could not see water anywhere or even where it might come from. Wondering keen, he thought about putting a question on the why of the bridge, sat, as it was, against the where of the water to one of the few early risen locals who were to be seen wandering around. But with a second thought, he reckoned it would be a better thing than not to appear at ease rather than to hop and to shout in a new come show. And so, instead, he walked some way up a different street to the one he had walked down where he then stopped to sit his bones on a wooden seat, under the branches of a large chestnut tree. To be sat, where he was, gave him a wide angle view to watch as the people of Crowland came out of their houses to make a start on the day at a going pace that seemed neither hurried nor slow but which moved through their arms, their hands and through their legs, lifting up their feet and nodding their heads, as each and all of them went on doing what there was to be done. The fact that from where he was sat he could see better than he could hear brought a small flash of annoyance to his brain, causing him to lean forward with his best pin sharp ear, keening to know the exact words which were spoken between the talkers he saw. What he *could* hear was only a snatch of a sound, a low sung voice, the clink of bottles, the jangle of keys, the scraping of boots and the creaking of doors. As he sat, with a lean, he was caught in the brain with the sudden realisation that if he was eager to speak to those he could for the time he was there, he ought to come, at least, to a slight understanding of how he might do it. Over to the left of his seat he could see a large wooden trapdoor set into the ground some way out in the open from the nearest house. Such a position made for a somewhat odd positioning of it, seeming, as it did, to have had less than more of a reason to have been put where it was by whom so ever had chosen to do so. Peering closer through half closed eyes, Woller noticed a sliver of yellow bulbed light coming from the inside. In addition to which he could hear the feint carried sounds of a conversation, one which he decided it would be a better thing than not for him to get a gist of. Accordingly, by means of sauntering across and flattening his bones down against the wood of the door itself, with his head held at a listening angle to the words to be heard, getting a gist with a listening ear was easy enough done. What do you want to know? asked Milo. It would be better if you could just tell me, said Cornelius Karp. About what? asked Milo. About the man you saw, said Cornelius Karp. I don't even know him, said Milo. There are some who reckon you spoke to him around the time of the unusual events at Pode Hole, said Cornelius Karp. Who told you that? asked Milo. It doesn't matter who told me, said Cornelius Karp. It matters to me, said Milo. It was just something I heard, said Cornelius Karp. Then where did you hear it? asked Milo. Good question, said Cornelius Karp. Are you saying you don't remember where it was? asked Milo. Something like that, said Cornelius Karp. So how can you be sure you heard the words in the correct order, if you cant even recall where you were, when you thought you heard them? asked Milo. I don't know how to explain it, said Cornelius Karp. Meaning, you know only what you thought you heard, at the time you were there, said Milo. Exactly, said Cornelius Karp. Wherever it was, said Milo. Yes, said Cornelius Karp. Curious, said Milo. More to the point, said Cornelius Karp, you still haven't told me whether or not you spoke to the man. I haven't, said Milo. So, is it true? asked Cornelius Karp. Yes, said Milo. Tell me about it then, said Cornelius Karp. What, all of it? asked Milo. All of it, said Cornelius Karp, the how and the why and the when of it. Well yes, I saw him but it was not deliberate, said Milo. What do you mean by that? asked Cornelius Karp. It was a fleeting moment of seeing, said Milo. A sighting, said Cornelius Karp. Quite, said Milo. Continue, said Cornelius Karp. I am not sure I can remember, said Milo. When was this then? asked Cornelius Karp. It must have been sometime last week, down by the curving bridge at Parson Drove, said Milo. As you were walking from Murrow, said Cornelius Karp. Well yes, said Milo. Can you remember how he looked? asked Cornelius Karp. He looked exactly as such a man would look, said Milo. What was he doing? asked Cornelius Karp. I don't know, he was just standing there almost under the bridge, staring at the water, said Milo. But you did speak to him, said Cornelius Karp. Well only sort of, said Milo. What do you mean, only sort of? asked Cornelius Karp. I was not sure what to say to him, said Milo. Was there anything unusual about about the way in which he was staring at the water? asked Cornelius Karp. It looked as though he was searching for something, said Milo. Maybe he is still looking for the meedler vong, said Cornelius Karp. Could be, said Milo. Was he still there when you last saw him? said Cornelius Karp. He had barely moved when I left, said Milo. So what did he tell you before then? asked Cornelius Karp. Something about the fennermarsh people suffering from confusion, said Milo. I assume you are talking about those who were caught up in the unusual events at Pode Hole? I am, said Milo. Did he say how many were confused? asked Cornelius Karp. No more than three and none of them seriously, said Milo. And are all of them are recovered now? asked Cornelius Karp. So he said, said Milo. Strange, said Cornelius Karp. I know, said Milo, although, no one seems to know how bewildered they were. Are you saying there is no point in asking? asked Cornelius Karp. What do you think? asked Milo. I think you could tell me about Orange Orlando, said Cornelius Karp. I have no idea who you mean, said Milo. Don't come your cross eyed look with me, he must be familiar to you, said Cornelius Karp. Does he have orange hair? asked Milo. I don't think he does, said Cornelius Karp. Orange Orlando, you say? asked Milo. Yes, said Cornelius Karp. Without Orange hair, said Milo. Yes, said Cornelius Karp. Sounds a peculiar finking sort, don't you reckon? asked Milo. It's a point of view, said Cornelius Karp. Woller pulled his ear away from the wood of the large trapdoor. Then, pushing himself up on his hands, he got back on his feet again. After which he took a stride in his shoes back to the street, where he then stood for some time, staring out, as he pulled with one hand at his hair, while, with the other, he rubbed at his chin, as he thought for a moment about what he had seen. And about what he could see, of those who called

Crowland a home of their own. What he could remember more than anything else from his earlier being learned, was that no attention had ever been paid to the right way or the wrong way of the mattering means, as suggested for each and all of the fennermarsh people throughout the wider fen lands. Those who had turned themselves up in the town, losing out and clappered fast, were encouraged to lose their concern with a suggestion that there was almost no matter to be lost, when nothing could be taken. Woller was minded to think that for some, this way of being could, more often than not, be seen as something about which there was much to admired. While, at other times, it could be taken as a threat to be seen off, as something that would whirl into motion with a quick time stamping of forms and of boots, a cracking of bones and a cleaning of thoughts, depending on the circumstances at the time. It seemed to those in Crowland that a better than otherwise way of doing the done thing was for them to smile when they could, for as long they could do so. As such, it was not a stretch of the imagination for Woller to recognise a common line of thinking that if the choosing of their behaviour was taking shape at a remove from their own raising of an opinion, then whatever was chosen, by them, would be of a less than effective held worth. With this much understood, the Crowlanders themselves concluded that to live however they could, whenever they could, was the thing to be done. On the follow of his sudden decision, at the beginning of the day, to boot up and leg it over the fen to a place where he hoped he could be more at ease with his thoughts, Woller could feel, within his own known self, an enveloping sense of relief to be free from all he was sure had been weighing on his thirst gripped brain. Even the morfiner juice seemed to sluice back through him as it had earlier done, pushing him off, in a stare of boggling eyes, as he stood in the street, goggling at the people he saw. And bending his ears too, at the sounds that came from in and around them, from the dinner shops and the greasers and the barkers and the boozers. Woller was minded to think of this as a good thing. As he stood where he was, with only the sense that for the moment, he was not sure where he was or even much caring of it either, he wondered about Samuel Amerson Averson, the occasional occupant of an old broken barn which had been long time abandoned, at the base of a bank, on the edge of Crowland Wash. He tried to remember something he had read, a piece or other of articled scutter, in the reckoning words of the scrawlers who worked on an enquiring journal. At the core of the scrawl was an assertion that Samuel Amerson Averson was close to the cut, sharpening edge of a fast come movement. One of the hurling burl and the whirling skirl, the newer than new, made better than ever before. Only he and his own brain were able to do what it was that the one or the two of them did. Sooner and not later after these words were seen, by those in search of a leading run, there was a collective banging of heads to suggest that this was a piece to be had, as across the fen lands, the hollering of louder voices was a starter to be heard. Some of them, with as loud a yelling sound as the voices of those who were were fond of their own hollering claims, were to be among the first of those knowers to know. And who pushed with a kick, the newest of the new things to happen. While, with a noise of their own, there were others still who had hollered the assertion that they ought to be seen against those scrawlers who were not aware of and could, therefore, not be trusted, with the newness of things. The argued hurl of the actual versus the abstract was joined in a quick time flash, by voices which were both quiet and restrained. And also by voiced opinions which were as loud as they were noodled, without slackening off or slowing on down. Over to one side of the scrawling fray, those finkers who could

agree to say something or anything better than nothing at all,
thought that Samuel Amerson Averson was of the same minded
thinking about the immediate concern to find a new idea for
the fennermarsh people, in order to alter their own perception
of themselves. All were sort of agreed that of the means which
were there to be seen, a choice would need to be made between
being as they were, waiting for change or mending what was
broken. Samuel Amerson Averson was well reckoned on the
latter course coming sooner than later. And to publish his
worded ideas in a new manifesto. One which was held by the
cultural elites of Gosberton Clough and Tydd Gote to be an
extraordinary document of commendable comprehension. A
piece of creative finking which was then without match in the
development of new thoughts. Samuel Amerson Averson was a
finker of an unusual sort who followed his own line at all times,
being, as he was, of the opinion that for some time a gradual
awakening had been taking place in the minds of the
fennermarsh people. They had become aware of what the
mattering means were. And with this would come mutual
recognition leading, eventually, to concerted action. A whole
new way of thinking had become possible, bringing into
common usage the methods and techniques with which each
and all in the flat lands could resolve the problems of adapting
themselves to their environment in a new, conscious and
creative way. A new association of a fennermarsh sort was
envisaged for those who were concerned to articulate an
effective strategy for a new way of doing whatever needed to be
done – a society for curious thought to foster the very idea of
curiosity. And also notions of finking discovery, in what
Samuel Amerson Averson hoped could be the pursuit of a
better made future for all those scattered across the wider fen
lands. The common interests of the fennermarsh people would
be well served through what he conceived as a community of

the mind, a finking association independent of the cultural elites of Gosberton Clough and Tydd Gote. One which could create a fertile ambience for new knowledge, in which the best of what was thought and imagined could flourish. A society for curious thought could consult with both individual and collective means, enabling those involved to create a new kind of knowing matter, to think in all directions, to reflect on their own experiences. And consider their aspirations. There were moments when Samuel Amerson Averson thought he was less than more sure he could do what he wanted to do, unless he could encourage the creation of a continuous experiment where no one would be in control or excluded from the curious process, especially not those with a keening for the new which made now seem like then. To create a laboratory of ideas, was a close moving, though long held wont, where he hoped assumptions about reality and its implied constraints were no longer operative. What was essential, he said, before setting it down in his own scrawling hand, was a new sense of community as a regenerative force; an organisation of infinite elasticity which creative finking intelligence could soon enough recognise and engage with. It must be seen as a communal affair, he thought. And not least, it was suggested by some that there would be more than less of a keening need amongst the discoverers, the chin rubbers and the head scratching searchers for a lean to a keener way of being without a caring regard for the speed of cracking ends.

Ha hum, thought Woller, as he wondered whether or not
he ought to tie up the loosened laces on his shoes and push
himself out across the fen, home to his four storey town house
with the three, deep grey, almost black, painted front doors.
Otherwise, he could stay where he was, to see more than he had
seen of Crowland and those who were there, with their earlier
raised abbey which sat only a throw of a stone from the peculiar
bridge. Hum ha, he thought. And he was about to decide on
the matter, when sudden quick time, with no hint of a warning,
he was caught by a whacking blow from the inside of his own
sack of bones. As ever, this loosened their shape and wracked
him double at the crack of the pain, felling him sharp in a drop
to his knees. With a leaning effort, he tried to stand, first on
one foot and then on the other. But the hurting was too much
to take, causing him to slump down again in the street, where
he was and stick a rummaging hand in a pocket of his coat to
find a bone numbing shot of his morfiner juice. Aah noo wah,
he said to himself, as he sank his worn matter deep into his
coat. Woller knew from his own gone times that it would be
a better thing than not if he could move himself inside, to lie
his bones flat on the floor, for as long as it might take for the
cracking to stop. And so he did, crawling on his belly through
an almost closed gate in a wall that was less than more of a way
from where he had been slumped, from the earlier falling crash.
Shutting the gate from the inside, he heaved his wracking bones
to lie in a curl against the wall. With his coat pulled over his
head, he waited in hope for a moment of ease which then stole
through the quiet of his mind, stilled and softening as it was,
in the weak light of the morning, leaving him content only to
be. As he was absent mindedly looking at the letterbox fixed
close to the ground in the wood of the gate, there was a bang
out of nowhere and he was struck with a starting jolt by a hard,
banging crash from the outside which shook the hinges as it

came. Knowing he could not for the moment move while also being less than more keen to do so, Woller made no attempt to reach out a hand, to the latch, to open the gate. Whatever it was out there in the street, on the outside, it might also be something or someone he wanted nothing to with, causing him to bury his face further into his coat and thrust a finger, in each of his ears, to block out the noise. Sitting, as he was, in the dark, he was rocked with surprise at the realisation that he had heard the sound of the gate crash banger before, somewhere that was elsewhere. The shouting he could now hear, coming from the other side of the gate, was the same as the sort which had come from out and within cousin Wilomena, though, stranger still, she was not a cousin of his. And he had not known her well. Cousin Wilomena, however, seemed to be a cousin to someone or other. And the sound of her voice was familiar enough from his meeting her, on several occasions, through Thelonius Greeling, who had invited her to various parties of the private gathering kind at his red brick town house on the river Nene. As he listened to her now, Woller also recalled that she had somehow been involved with blue eyed Basil. Whatever the arrangement had been, though, it had leaped, in a yelling of words and a smashing of plates, out of the control of either of the two, each and the other, due to a soon come temper, she, for the most part, held in herself. One, however, which could sheer off loose in a rush. Dazed as he was for a clear thought to form in his morfiner juiced mind, Woller tried to picture a face, before letting it go, when the only thing he could haul into his remembering was an image of a woman in a long blue dress. And even this was guessed at with what had been his memory, shot through with holes as it seemed to be, aside from the triggers that flew sparks in his brain, such as the colour of a dress and where it was worn. Woller yelled out through the letterbox. Cousin Wilomena shouted back. And so, through the confusion of their bellowed words in what seemed a strange method, to both he and she, they succeeded in holding a conversation of sorts. It took only a small amount of yell, bellowing, shouting to realise that she had turned up at the wrong gate, looking for someone else other than him, though she did not say which might have been the right gate or even who she was looking for. And neither did he ask or talking tell her who he was. For a beat, there was silence, before cousin Wilomena cleared her throat, apologised through the letterbox for the intrusion and was gone.

Sitting on a chair at his desk, on the top floor of the four storey town house with the three, deep grey, almost black, front doors, Woller soon started in on a head scratching noodle of a think. He wondered how he could use the words which were circling around on both the inside and the outside of his own mind to make a new work which would glean, with a keening ease, an answer to the question of being, seeing and hee hee heeing, as well as one which would also be recognisable to his friends and those who knew him. And not only to them but also to those throughout the wider fen lands who might hope to see their own selves reflected, on hearing their singular tales told. There were times when he would talk out loud to no one else but himself, so that he could listen to the sounds of his own finking. And sometimes, he would scrawl down the words of his reasoned explanation for the genesis of the new work. But at other times, he would claim, to those who were listening when he began, with a surprising cough, to speak, he had only considered starting in on such a piece as a means to escape from the part scrawled down, clackerack idea he had been working on earlier before. An idea that could still be used to chuck a hooking stop against his tendency to forget more than less of the mattering means of his friends, those who knew him and those who did not. The new work on which Woller had decided he would pull a chair up to his desk and be sat there until it was complete, was a scrawl of words to be acted on by one of a company of bawling squawlers. As the telling of it had been with him for a long time gone, a calling name was then coming to a better made shape in his brain. And this, was Joller the swoondler. Whenever he was asked about the how and the why of a scrawling call, he would only say that the why and the how, of such a thing, as the calling of well scrawled words, was for no other reason that it was – or might be, at least, he thought to himself. And with no further explanation from him to anyone else, that seemed to be that. As he sat, with the pages he was wanting to fill, fat and full with his own ink, scrawl finking, Woller found himself thrown back in his chair when he realised the ease with which the words were leaking from his brain and down onto the paper. Continuing without a break, it seemed his scrawling hand was moving sharp time quicker than he could ever have imagined, especially when beginning a new work that was still less than much of a notion on the inside of his crack boned head. One which was, for a finker, a harder understanding to reach than most, in terms of how he might come across such a surprising development that did not involve a large degree of chin rubbing, head scratching, hair pulling and foot stomping. Along with a hurled yelling of yelled out words at the page, at the chair, at the walls and at his own finking self. Minded, as he then was, in a boomers charge, he could not even begin to know what or where the matter might be, whether in the lacking hollow of a cracking in the brain or a reasonable, rational way of being, of sitting, of scrawling and of staring at the wall. What he saw as a liberation, in the scrawling down of Joller the swoondler, was a thing that wheeled freer than ever he could have thought. And when he weighed up the bones in his hands, Woller reckoned that the doing of it was enough to catch the cracks running though his brain before they ran off without stopping. A bonus to be added was that for those who would claim a responsible hand in making the right decisions and not the wrong ones, the interests of Joller the swoondler were straight off boggling to their collective dog eared sensibilities. As a consequence of this, the confusion was greater than some were expecting, when nothing was said and nothing was done, nothing was decided and no conclusions were drawn. Woller assumed that one other factor, in the wider reasoning of some, could be the result of the contents of the worded scrawl only having been read by a few of those with concerns about the words to be used. Although, any clammer bang, over and gone despair was heaved out of the way by an even more peculiar laughing smiler from among the chosen bawling squallers. But then, it was considered by most that one of Wollers qualities as a scrawler was his way with a har de har guffaw which would come leaping out from the page, to go fizzing off in the words of his speakers, even as they hauled themselves through, as low as a bag of loose hanging bones could go. And it seemed to some who had read the new work that his talent for comedic desperation was more to be seen than it had ever been before, in a fetter free, broken loose pondering on the worst that could be thought, by those who had taken a fall, hard enough to be trodden in, with the knowing of it for themselves. The wearing down of despair, in the thoughts and the words, sometimes scrawled and at other times not, was pondered without the slack of a reasoning lack or the reasoned shouting of an argued stand. The happening means of passing through, of going around and about in the time that was spent, by those who would spend it however they could, was a thing he recognised as a significant matter to be knocked on the head. And on occasion, more than less time was spent needling a way through the course of a clattering game or a wall staring moment.

Joller the swoondler was a friend to be had, someone to be trusted, as he put his trust in his friends and those who knew him. The importance to him of making a contribution, of making an effort and to be seen doing *something* was a deal of a thing. And in the same vein, as much of it and more was to be known in a way that was free of the fat on the bones of congratulation. The way that he was, the way that he saw who he was, made for a method in his own mind that pushed him on wide and open. There might also have been a twist in the need to look too hard, at what some considered to be, a degree of grace in his character. And even though a fashioning of humility was an earlier and different thing, it had less of a meaning depending on who the fashioner was. An understanding of it was contingent too, on thinking about those who were expected to wear that which had been created for them. But in spite of the whatever and the whenever of the issues at hand, if a swerving glide could be made, off to one side, it would be done with a question or more to be asked about what it was and what it wasn't to be a humble down man. The own known behaviour of Joller the swoondler was an illustration of how his talent for endearing himself to the fennermarsh people was all to the good for the art of the swoondling sort, convinced in his own mind, as he was, from the beginning that he could and would set his feet down at their best. And also, his legs and his hips and his chest and his arms, as fair and as four square as he was able to do. Along with his neck and his throat and his tongue in his head that sat on the top of his hanging bones. It was known by his friends, those who knew him and by the fennermarsh people that more than a deal of much had happened to Joller the swoondler from the start, through a stumbling muddle, to the point he was at, though, of the chew of the means to be known, there was no more than there was. To know there had been meaning, was not the same as knowing just what the matter was. And that seemed to be that. But for those who were keen on a close in look at the weave of it all or to pull at the seams, there was a wont to get more, to hum ha ponder on the why and the when. Still, it could be seen easy enough that for all those who were keening sharp, there was more often than not one who was less so. Joller the swoondler was, however, quicker off the swoondling mark than most, cutting fast through the tape with his poorly head shrinking. At the time, he had jumped straight up and hopping with a fine reckoned notion, a plan of sorts. While this could have been described as being well drawn, it was barely carried on from much more than the lowest form of planning required for such a notional scheme. And though it had earlier seemed like a runner, he thought it through as he often did, with a rub of his chin and a scratch at his head, as he paced up, down and around in a spin, before falling to the floor in a curl of a shape, slipped off in a sleeper to think harder and deeper. And in so doing, his thinking had convinced him that he could indeed release the means from actual events and therefore, from mere mattering function. As an idea, he found this exhilarating, giving, as it did, his swoondling work a feverish new clarity. This work was wide owned in its questioning of the brain and the bones which all of the finkers were in. In his role as a swoondler this was something he knew about, stuck grumping, as he had long been, in a sack of loose hanging bones of his own. As such, he owed much to the becoming frailty of being, intrigued, as he was, by how matter was manoeuvred, how it could seem and be seen. He just wanted to know, he said. It was easier to be brought down in a bruised thump of a whack than it was to find comfort for the mind and the feet, as the bruising and the whacking could come sudden quick, with no hint or a warning about when or from where. What he most wanted was that which he had worked hardest to conjure and make real, to exist in more than his own brain as a shaping of his peculiarly minded imagination. Without wishing for magic to seep in, through hard boned heads and bone headed thoughts, he was aware that as a swoondler at large, all he could see was that there were no rules. It was this which allowed him to do what he would. And what he could, whenever he wanted, hauling the swoondlers art up to heights that had never before been reached, to somewhere that was elsewhere, in the minds of those who were smaller than him. There were words scrawled down to the effect that he gave swoondling a power and a strength the fennermarsh people assumed it already had, a long time before then. As it stood, he was far from a teller of how it was done, going only so far to suggest that a core of the meaning was a personal thing. And exactly how someone might be affected by a swoondle was contingent on their own knowing condition at the time it was done. His own curious appetites were insatiable, wanting it all, as soon as it was there to be had. No matter how complex the swoondle, the particularities that were involved were invariably harmonised to give those who were present an experience of complete coherence. Joller the swoondler wore his much vaunted knowing easier than most. And while his swoondling work was known as a brightener of minds and a lighter of needs, it was recognised too that it was looser than some with a pull on the cord. What he seemed to offer the fennermarsh people was a slow taken smile and a catch in the throat, though, where the vulnerability sat was something that left even him at a loss. Whatever it was that he gave, it would be a hook to a sharp thinking hooker for immediate access to the swoondlers art, even for those who were encountering it for the first time. With regard to his working practice, he was industrious, though not overly so, being prolific but not simply a machine that spewed forth the swoondling means as a way in which to

construct an approach to his work. And the way his mind
worked was no different to his understanding of the means
which mattered, seeing as he was less interested in grand set
pieces than the incidental detail that combined to form a whole,
as he engaged with and observed the fennermarsh people and
the imagery that pitched in on his brain. While recognising
that visual language could become distorted, he was also aware
that it could be precise, thinking that it could distort *in order to
be precise*. And in his hands, it was used to devastating effect.
There were some situations in which Joller the swoondlers first
principle was to observe enough to make sense of the stories
which were threaded through the course of swoondling history,
to then be added to his readings of the past, even though these
could not be confused with actual events. Joller the swoondler,
nonetheless, reckoned that he ought to offer the fennermarsh
people their own tall tale tellings, so that the look of their
reflections could be found. All he asked in return was that on
hearing and seeing each and all of his well honed tales, they
decide for themselves. With this in mind, he decided on telling
them his own version of the history of the fennermarsh wars.
At the beginning of the cause of all the trouble, the fennermarsh
people stood at a point where they had to choose between one
thing and another, either anarchic moodling or authoritarian
booming. And the direction and goal of this period of change
sooner and not later became a matter of intense dispute, one
which eventually spilled over into open clattering conflict. The
fennermarsh people, their fears exploited by those who knew
better, took to the fields and the streets, as their formerly
understood notions collapsed in the face of the sudden come
raising of arms, accompanied by louder heard shouts than
before. The tearing down of all that was familiar, soon after
this, quick enough led to the emergence of two opposing
clattering groups, in the form of the moodlers and the boomers.

The first clashes between the two were then reported, with the final escalation towards all out clattering beginning when some among the moodlers convinced those boomers, who had wavered between peace and conflict, to support the latter. As a result, the first serious clatterings were fought at the end of the month. At the start of the conflict, the front line ran through the open fields from Clay Hole House in the east to Swineshead Low Ground in the west, dividing the fen lands into a moodler and a boomer of a place, with the boomers controlling the area to the south while the moodlers controlled all the land to the north. Although even then, enclaves of the opposing forces existed on both sides of the line, meaning that mutual elimination of these was a priority. The moodlers seized the initiative, taking control of large swathes of territory across the northern fens. A chronic shortage of skilled leaders, however, left them unable to capitalise on their initial momentum. Consequently, most of their offensives came to nothing. The core strategic manouvre of the leather coat wearing General from Amber Hill was to launch a diversionary attack at Swineshead, while at the same time advancing along a line through Wigtoft fen to the north and north west of Sutterton. The moodlers collapsed under the weight of the assault, some of them retreating in panic as far north as Witham Marsh. After their defeat, the moodlers legged it up and off, leaving the boomers in almost complete control. The clattering was a catastrophe for the fen lands with many killed or disappeared and it, therefore, seemed a sensible enough thing to send someone out from the mess of it all to find a better way of being, for moodlers and boomers the same. This someone was Joller the swoondler, according to him at least. Although, in spite of what he claimed were his starting aims, the forcing in deep of a long scratched idea was thought not to be a part of his swoondling work. As a matter of fact he said, it was rather the opposite. What he offered was the opportunity to glimpse a fennermarsh land. One that was thrown in and turned, spun on the up and dropped on its side. A place that could be sunk, clunked and junked without cause for concern. With Joller the swoondler, the meaning of things was often different to what it had earlier been. At times, it seemed that what was meant would be changed from was to was not which was confusing and wonking for those who were there when the swoondling was done. All that he left, when he had cleaned out and gone, was a lurch of the familiar, the creation of a swoondled fink, slower timed blinking and learning to be. He took this as he found it woven into his work, knowing that he was capable of swoondling meaning from wherever it could be swoondled without resorting to the sentimental ideal of a sweetened past. On no occasion, when dealing with the question of what it was to be made in a man shaped bag, hung loose on bones and with a pulsing flow, did he start on in with a wider wrought theme, as this would be at the expense of what it was to breathe, to move, to think and to see, he thought. All he wanted was to know his friends and those who knew him better than he did, keen as he was for them to know more of themselves than the gush of blood and the flail of limbs. On the occasions when it was obvious enough that the mass of the fennermarsh people were off too soon and hurtling quick, clashing, colliding and tearing down their means in a maddening rush, his own ways of dealing with them were far from brutal, he claimed. On the contrary, he found the anarchic tumbling intriguing, rather than a concern to be had, he said. What could not be seen from without was the enormous strength and endurance of the swoondling man who had a uniquely collected and compact nature which enabled him to swoondle a large amount from whatever he had. And all the while, it might have appeared as though he had never really tried. Joller the swoondler often revealed his flashing humour through the work and in his own self too, being less than more afraid of his own weaknesses and vulnerabilities than most. On the occasions when he took on such a role, he was an inspirational teacher; flamboyant and incisive, he could convey knowledge and encourage those in his charge with enviable ease. A common notion had long been held that there was not a trace of arrogance to be seen, with some accounts noting a humble quality to his expression, his eyes appearing soft and curious. What all were certainly agreed on was that precision and the pursuit of perfection were ideals to which he returned again and again. An assumed personal style, combined with a professional rigor, was, however, given room to breathe as a carrier for other gotten qualities such as irony and suggestiveness which imbued his swoondling with soul. As he was without expectation it, therefore, followed that the response of the fennermarsh people was not something to be anticipated, he thought. Each and all were free from manipulation and sentimental direction, he said. At no time were they told what and how to think, he insisted. Joller the swoondler worked hard to ensure there was depth to his work without the need for unnecessary confusion of the swoondlers art, though there was at least some complexity to it which was widely acknowledged to be a good thing. And more than most would have thought, he was pleased with his reputation as a swoondler who was both out on his own and respected by the scrawling finkers (he knew it was so). As a consequence of this, he also enjoyed popular acclaim which was a feat he considered to be rare enough. Joller the swoondler could indulge his need for his friends and those who knew him in a direct connection with everyone and anyone else, through being able to reinforce this with an elegant swoondling virtuosity. The collective appreciation of the fennermarsh people with whom he worked was plain to see. Although, to have removed the layers would have brought an expectation of finding something that might have been better not found. Joller the swoondlers public tone was one of warmth and well meaning. And even his teeth bearing was of considerable charm, calming and welcoming too. Each and all would be considered and recognised, though not at the expense of his own brained understanding of the space between them and him. Clarity was the only thing he wanted, he knew that. There was no vanity or neurosis in his own self. Well, was there, he asked? Surely he said, there could be nothing more to his own means than a beguiling honesty. While he was no stranger to the absurd, this did not translate to the swoondling itself in an obvious or expected manner. Absurdity was comic ha ha or tragi – hoo comic ha. All of which meant that a sense of tragedy in the purest of forms was not to be found. But then, what was tragedy anyway? This was a question he asked more than most, arguing that everything was open to interpretation. The experience he had was readily apparent, as were the demands on him as a swoondler. But his talent for swoondling was not about what the fennermarsh people might possibly have been like – he was interested in wider held notions. Although even this seemingly simple proposition was fraught with problems. Some finkers such as Doctor Mungo would argue that the only wider held notion was the smile which likewise became problematic with regard to approaching a swoondle. As with all wider held thought, it could be argued that there were no absolutes which was to say that no two finkers would ever look at a swoondle in exactly the same way. In the mind of a seeker of free association such as he was, this was for Joller the swoondler a good thing. In a similar vein, he was a scorner of artifice who chose to take an approach which brought what he called a natural elegance to the fore. And though there were some who could not be sure what such a thing might be, *he*

claimed it was the key to all he had done. It was the starter for every move he made, he said. And this elegance could become either epic both in scale and concept or it could be positioned opposite and made more oblique and intimate. One of his favourite acts was to fuse fact with fiction, which indulged the imagination of the fennermarsh people while challenging the expectations of his friends and those who knew him.
Sometimes, he would even make a pretence of becoming his own fictional character, one that could serve to transport those who were swoondled to situations which would otherwise have been impossible for them to experience. The connection for Joller the swoondler was between the swoondlers art and the mattering means. And how to bridge the gap for the fennermarsh people. As a swoondler he was alive to his themes, with images of his work being open to all those who saw it. He was not a control freak, was his insistent refrain. And neither did he make elaborate allusions to himself in his swoondling. Those who were often included in his work were all authentically idiosyncratic rather than merely representative of wider characteristics. The calling of his swoondling, the saying of it and the knowing of it by his friends, those who knew him, the finkers and the fennermarsh people was of major significance because it underpinned the motivation he had for each and every new swoondle. Concerned with subverting the orthodox scowl he was a most singular swoondler. The look of a swoondle of his was known to be unique and without equal in any regard, even though this was not deliberate but was simply a thing that had happened through his own curious application of the swoondlers art. And although this was not something at which he railed, he was less than more keen to insulate himself within his own peculiar practice, aware as he was that his aim had always been to turn his mind to his work in such a way that it would be consistently greater than the sum of its parts which

was to give the swoondlers art a dash that was both relevant and resonant. It seemed to him that insulation became solipsism, became isolation and he was a worrier against creating a persona for nothing more than public consumption. If one *were* to be created, however, there was not much which could be done to quieten it down. Joller was a swoondler in his bones as much as in his brain, as one balanced the other without causing the work to become lost from the essence of what it was, what he wanted it to be. And even what he thought it ought to be. The fennermarsh people were of the opinion that the ideal was for him to be more distinct than most in his own shown self with the branding seen as fundamental to his swoondling soul, in order to load the work with a feeling that could be and was felt. It was not a static conceit but an evolving pattern with the familiarity of his methods facilitating communication and continuity, making it possible for the swoondler to be what he was in spite of the fact that there were those who were using language and firm shoved materials of whatever sort which were robust enough to cope with any amount of elaboration. And it was a quick done thing to forget that to hook on a tag to mark the swoondling as it was done, was less of a concern than the elegance, the sensibility, the branding and the handling of the language as it was used. All of which combined to make the nominal physical identity a long gone thing, in known finking terms at least. The tagging of a swoondle by those who had no understanding of the methods which were used was thought to be a looping idea, fit for nothing but selling on quick, not least by some for whom finking ways were thought to be essential when conjuring with the scrawlers of the fink. The result of this was that Joller the swoondler seemed energised to invest his swoondling work with as much of his own mattering means as he could, to lend the art of the swoondle a new meaning, while becoming less than more concerned about losing out to a complacent enthusiasm. There were some ideas which he recognised as worthy of serious consideration. There was also hard work, the graft and grit to be gotten through. Joller the swoondler was, however, neither pious nor puritanical. What he *could* be though, was a thirster for commitment, imagining as he did that he was free of the ego that could accompany this. The volume of the hum ha thinking he did had the effect of opening up wider horizons to be seen by the fennermarsh people, some of whom were set on sharing with him a tongue to tell the tales that were told, to make with the swoondling as a curious pursuit of the mattering means. Although he saw little point in attaching significance to objects of shape but no beat, he was keener than most to create the circumstances in which his swoondling success would soon enough become the cruncher for numbers in clean, cashed up terms. Other than this, there was an aversion of sorts in his mind to clinging on hard to matter which made him curiously homeless, as with no attachment to material things he could be free of the need to keep a clutching hold on a key to a front door of his own. The notion of home was for him a sentimental one with any place incurring such a label being no more or less arbitrary than the next, leaving him nowhere and everywhere. At ease with being in his own wrapped skin, Joller the swoondlers lack of faith in much other than his own means allowed him to see others as carriers of nothing more than a bulk of bone to be broken down, sent on their way and gone to the sound of a har de har har. The same ought to go for the brain, he thought. Along with a finking core which some considered to be not much given to a learning move. In his own mind, the losing of matter did not translate as a clang on a bell so much as a terror of suffering from rotten decay, like a slow wearing away of weakening flesh. What could be easier to understand, he asked, than a lingering thought? Hum ha, said the fennermarsh people with a single voice. In contrast, all he could say was ha hum, being as he was of the opinion that he had come too close to lose what remained of a hurtling need. This was not to deny the value of pausing or taking stock but was a recognition of wanting more than could be gained through knowledge at the expense of searching for better returns, as when knowing was used for no other purpose than vain decoration it could only become redundant. Some might have said that his wide held arms and his tooth white grin made him a constructive supporter when it came to a swoondled collaboration. And although it was a lesser thing than otherwise for him to do to take much of a swoondle outside his own personal swoondling, he, nonetheless, placed a rare value on the opportunity, committing himself with a keening lead to any such venture. Joller the swoondler was enthusiastic about notions of fate. And so the notion of the swoondler monk, a paragon of virtue and worth all his salt, sat churning his hands and his thoughts through a wrestle of work to be done, in search of a better place than the place he was in, was neither appealing or convincing. Considering this to be the behaviour of the over zealous, he had no wish to be saddled, bitted and hauled somewhere other than he thought he ought to be. And because he had no sense of a greater vision made manifest on an epic scale, his swoondles were within reach of all the fennermarsh people. And all the fennermarsh people were within reach of all his swoondles, not least because he had something to offer as well as something to take. There were some who thought that Joller the swoondler was complete, peerless and transcendental. There were those who asked the question, was Joller the swoondler real or imagined? There were others still who were less than more sure about asking questions of any sort. All he said in response was that at no time would he be looking to encourage flattering opinion, knowing well how fleeting the effects would be. Some

of the finking sort thought of his swoondling work as being
without concern for wider opinion, looking only to the new
and the next to be known. Conjecture was not, however,
imagination or hypothesis. It was something seedier, needier,
weighted with expectation, he said. Joller the swoondler had no
expectations, either of the fennermarsh people or his
swoondling work, as it was what it was. And what it could and
would be, he claimed. That Joller was a swoondler who saw
himself as free without the burden of a need to fumble and
grumble, was a good thing for his swoondling because it
allowed the mattering means to breathe, to exist in their own
space on the inner most side of various minded thoughts.
There was a seamless progression of his ideas and swoondling
concerns in concert with the fennermarsh people, each and all
of whom were free to make their own decisions, he said. As
well as being capable of speaking his words with a finking turn,
Joller the swoondler could see them from deep down in,
meaning he was pleased to make connections of an emotional
sort even if this carried the risk of a crack to the brain and to
sudden come hurt. A sensitive man, he was reactive to the
thoughts and feelings of others, he knew that. Nothing was
imposed, he said, as the demands others made on him were to
be welcomed. By opening his mind to curious thoughts he
could become a better swoondler than ever, he hollered, in the
hope that he would, even as he wailed about a need for him to
engage the inner with the outer in each and every given
circumstance. While on the one hand he was aware of both har
de har and scared up frit visions of the condition he was in, it
seemed to some of those who were looking on that it would be
easy enough for him to lose a sense of balance when measuring
this against the ideals of a smiling world. One which he saw as
dog eared and pinned down with the wrong sort of thinking.
And therefore, by association, any characteristics were gathered

in as no more than a theoretical adjunct because research and statistics were rarely collected in the pursuit of objectivity, being used instead to support whatever thesis was on the end of a determined push. The meaning of Joller the swoondler was beginning to leak through the cracks, seeping out in a manner candid enough to be regarded as a laying bare of the self with an exposing of the nerves, of the raw cut fibres that smarted and fizzed, reacting to both the beautiful and the less so. What he could feel there and then, was more than most of his own scarce known means in the form of a swoondling language which was elegant and at one with a sensibility that belonged to no one but him. Joller the swoondler had dared to be and his daring would become genius.

Woller was more than a little aware that he had long time failed to take his hoped for, allocated lot as a sleeper, waking and staring as he had with goggle stalked eyes fixed on ceilings or roofs of the rusted tin sort, from as many beds or cold, hardened floors as he cared to remember. For the most part though, he had considered this sleeping lack to be benign rather than otherwise. And therefore, less than more of a cause for him to have reckoned it anything other than a frightened trembler of a short, bad dream, thrashed out beneath caught, tangled covers. He was, however, soon time struck with the not so fortunate happening of a headlong crash into a different way of being when he let his eyes close. Straight out of wherever and without even the smallest hint of a warning, he would find himself hurtling out of his sleeping self, thrown with a lurch and a head smack fall against a table, across a chair, crunching his means into matter that seemed to be everywhere or at least anywhere he might be, before standing at last to push his back against a wall in a desperate effort to earth his quivering sack of loose hanging bones, stood as he was on a lean of pressed palms, wet in a sweat, with both of his feet braced hard on the floor. Sometimes, he thought to fold himself over and slide down to a crouch. While at others, he strained in his brain to remember what he ought to do when the beat in his chest felt certain to burst, leaving his breathing gone for the count as he shook all alone in the dark, reaching out a fumbling hand to feel a familiar switch for the light. And waiting, either for suffocation or release. This, he was minded to think, could only be a bad thing. After a long scratch of his head, Woller came to the conclusion that he would reckon on it being a good thing if he could do something about his sleeping lack which would mean he would need to let go of the bit that was frit, coiled up between his ears. And also come to terms with losing use of his finking balance too, he thought. Wondering what to

do, he telephoned Orange Orlando to ask him if he might be
able to help. In the case of Orange Orlando, it was apparent
to his friends and those who knew him that his vocation as
a shrinker of poorly gone heads had been long time starting
and short time happening. With the rush he was in, however,
for the healing to start, Woller was keen enough to be given
advice, even if Orange Orlando was the only available mind
peering medicine man with a brain of good size in shrunken
head practice. All he could ask was that he might know what to
do. Orange Orlando talking told Woller on the end of the line
that he was a spring jumping enthusiast, as much as a keener
could be, for the opening up of cracked minds with the added
benefit of a rummage around inside by a qualified rummager
such as he was. And he there and then said he could promise
a cure, with a simple recommendation to an acquaintance of
his, a fellow jumper who would accept a referral from him,
if Woller would be pleased to be referred. Woller said that
he would. And so Orange Orlando suggested he get himself
over to Algakirk in the northern fens as quick as he could do
so. That a cut off somewhere out in the northern fens was the
place to be sent for a cure seemed a remarkable thing to Woller
when he thought on it some more. But then it could also be
said to make sense, if the talking words of Orange Orlando were
to be believed, as he had mentioned in brief that the shrinker
of poorly heads to whom he was being sent was himself a
remarkable individual of an extraordinarily original and even
controversial sort. Several years older than Woller but still
only in his first year of professional practice, the mind peering
medicine man had slip, staggered in on his own vocation
later than was recognised as the done thing. And that he had,
via a looping, no sense making route, when compared to the
experience of most of those in his profession only made him
less than more of an asset for a consultation in the sneering

opinion of his peering fellows. Although, for Woller, there was
not much about this of which he was concerned. It could be, he
thought, because his own need for the speed of the leaking self,
heal of a seal on his being how he was, was a cause for him to
decide without pause what to do. What he, therefore, decided
was to attend three consultations a week with the mind peering,
poorly head shrinking medicine man. He wondered whether
or not these would do him any helping good, a matter on which
he could not say either way. Still, he did know that the hurtling
out of his sleeping had come right on worse and he reckoned it
might be a good thing for someone else other than himself to
take a look through his ears to the inside of his brain, to have
a rummaging go at finding whatever it was that was in there,
causing him to shout. Then, with a sudden flash of an idea
which he could not be sure was a good one or not, he decided
on a rummage of his own before it might be established who
he was, when he had not even known who he had *been* without
a chance of a listening in on his own mattering means. In a
moment, he quick stuck a finger from each of his hands deep
in to each of his ears so that nothing could leak from the inside
to the outside, in order for him to listen hard to the far down
thoughts that were rumbling and grumbling at the back of his
own mind. After a long listening time, Woller slowly pulled
his fingers from out of his ears, stood up from where he had
been sat on the second floor landing at the top of the stairs of
his home loved home and looked at his watch with a quiet ha
hum to himself, as he noticed it was getting on for the end of
the afternoon. With a resolve to never make such a finger stuck
attempt again, he ran a hand through his hair while peering
out of the landing window to the front, wondering how little
or how much he was the same as those he might see out there
in the streets, those hoppers and shouters who had the most
to lose from an absence of free come thinking. With a rub of

a palm on the back of his neck, he hummed a ha of a catcher to know about a racing thought of the sort that concluded that if living were to be had, then he ought to be the first to get it as fast as he could, wherever, whenever and however it would come. Although, he was less than more sure about the speed that running bones were in need of reaching, to keep an even pace which could be held for a longer time than most without regard for whatever might be done to them or whatever they might do to themselves in the heat of the moment. This caused him to pause for a moment of his own minded thought on the question. When it eventually occurred to him that he might be stood where he was without ever finding the answer, it then seemed better to remove his head from the knock and look for his shoes instead. Woller was eager to find an easing way of warming his wrapper through, in and around a familiar pattern of the mattering means on either side of the only deep grey, almost black, painted front door which would open as it ought. He did not know, however, how such a thing could be achieved. At least, not in a way that was better than worse. And although he claimed to his friends and those who knew him that he had no preference for a particular side of the opening door to be closed, he knew he would take, if it were offered, the chance to close it from the inside and loosen his sack of bones into a heap in the empty hallway at the foot of the stairs. But not always alone. Noo wah, he thought.

Woller pulled an opening hand on the handle of the middle front door of three and stepped through to be stood on the outside in the street, just as the thin light was going. Despite the time of the year, the temperature had fallen to the point where all buttons, on all coats, were being buttoned over bones. While collars were being pulled over ears, hats were being pulled tight on heads, scarves were being wound around necks and tied about throats against the cut, slicing wind that hurtled across the flat land, tearing open the idle slack of those in its rush, caught fast and surprised to be so. Closing the door behind him, he pushed out his feet against the cold with a warming stomp of his shoes. And with a quickening snap of a wide arced flap with his arms, he legged it off and away from his peculiar house stood as it was in its odd looking street. As he tapped out a heel toed clack on the metalled path, Woller heaved in through his nostrils as deep a breather as he could, sucking in the air that he could barely smell and taste even less. All of which sent a smile curling up from the sides of his mouth for the briefest of moments, drawing it out from a sceptical blank to a slow creasing, hesitant smiler. A sort of smiling that went on until he turned a corner which sudden time quicker again, he reckoned he could have done without turning. In spite of not meaning to do so, he had walked himself straight into a wide, high sided alley filled black with a hanging, choking smoke that caught in his throat and stung in his eyes, needling hard when he coughed, as it sank with a lethal keeler in through his nose, down to his lungs and up to his brain. Twisting about in a frantic attempt to see if he could locate the source of the fink melting fumes that puthered and smoked and clung to his hair, he could hardly guess at where he was stood without hoping to find a starting flame or wherever it was they seemed to be fuming from, though with a blink of his fast watering eyes, he managed to snatch a look at the main billow of the choking stuff. He could see that it was not billowing out from down low by his knees but was coming from a height that was elsewhere, meaning it was the doing of those in the houses which each lined a back at the point where their bricks met to form the alley, wide and high sided as it was. With another blink and a glance he was able to note that along the length of each line of back facing houses he could see, there were the same built chimneys sat on the tops of the roofs. Underneath which were those he could blame for making themselves snug on the inside with the burning of coked junk in a grate against the cold while he flew mad on the outside, sooted and black. He coughed in the air that brought only burnt off fuel over rising fumes which weighed in his lungs, scaring him up to the peak of a frit sweat, as he could only stare with wet, boggling eyes at the filthy dark smoke that drew ever closer around him, no matter which way or when he was able to walk. Woller grabbed at his head with both hands when he felt it begin to knock away in a pounding fit, losing him what balance he had left. Then came a warping of his sight as the poisoned filth leaked into his brain, leeching his thoughts and crashing in on his own self, leaving only the basest of modes sparking and fizzing with life, causing him to stumble forward in his kiltered shoes, then almost down on his buckling legs in a near come panic where he caught a surge in his bones. And in a flashing yank of his jumper, up, over his head, he ran without breathing and less than much seeing, for what he hoped was the far end of the wide and high sided alley he was in. Gathering speed in a running go, he tripped and fell hard, cropping his stride in a flailing clatter of turned up heels as he landed in a tangle of wrists and shins, his head stuck in his jumper at an angled skew. As he lay where he was, feeling as he did the starting of a shake working a way though his aching, clattered bones, his first thought was for the smoke, wondering if he was still caught at the edge of its swirl or if he was now out of its reach. And more important than less, whether or not he could take a chance and push his head out for a breather of whatever it was that may well be out there waiting for him to do so. He stood himself up as the shape of man with no head. A shape that wobbled and swayed on the side of what it hoped was not an alley but a street in which at that moment, from the other end, a girl in a pair of pea green shoes came turning as she did, at the start of a walk of her own. On seeing what she saw, what she feared was the shape of a man with no head, she took a whack of a shock to her brain. Stopped fast in her stride, she was caught with a thought that for a girl such as she to be in the wrong place, at the wrong time, albeit with the right words and with some understanding, was a less than easy thing. But for a girl such as she to be in the wrong place, with the wrong words and with *no* understanding, was a barker of a bewildering thing to be missed even by those who wanted to miss nothing. The girl in the pea green shoes stood as she was in a half taken stride on the other side of the same street as the shape of man with no head was of a sudden come mind too far gone to clear. A goner even to focus on much other than the ease of the means that caused less and not more comment. Something which asked her only to expect the expected and the flat line quiet of being freed from concern. At no time had she been keen to be sudden and quick gog, boggling at a shape of a man which appeared to be standing as square as it could in its shoes while seeming confused by the lack of a head. As she stood on her side of the street and looked over the way, the shape of a man with no head seemed to be somewhat dazed as it began tentatively to flex both of its arms and both of its legs. And to feel each of its fingers on each of its hands, as if it were trying to make certain that everything was exactly where it had been not long before whatever it was that had happened to it had done so. When the

flexer seemed to be as pleased as it might be with the condition
of its own moveable parts, it hung its arms down by its sides
and waggled its hands as if it were wrestling with a decision on
what to do next. This was close to a question the girl in the pea
green shoes had put to herself. At the exact same moment and
still muffled inside the jumper, Woller reckoned it was worth a
chancing shot at a breather which even if turned out to be a bad
thing could only be a better thing than remaining as he was
with a gearing down of sensation and a balancing lack. He was,
however, less than much keen about poking his head out of the
jumper where he was stood or to move with his feet when he
could not even see further than a knotted pearl one. Minded, as
he was, to think that his aching bones were hurting with too
much of a crack for them to take another trip clattering fall, he
stood for a moment and waited, though for what he could not
have said. Then in a quickening flash with both hands, he
grabbed a hold on the collar of the jumper and pulled it down
hard as he jabbed his head through and out, snortelling in air
through his nose as he did so. With the realisation that he was
clear of the poisoning smoke, enough to take in a breather that
was as easy as it was deep, he felt a rush through his veins and
his brain of the relief he had earlier thought might never come.
At the same moment, he saw the girl in the pea green shoes on
the opposite site of the street stood staring straight at him with
gog boggled eyes. He looked at her while she continued to stare
at him. He smiled. She almost started in on a reactive smile but
a shriek came from out of her mouth instead. Then in a twist
of her hips and a lift of her feet, the girl in the pea green shoes
was off round the corner, gone in a scarpering dash. Woller was
inclined to decide against his legging it back through the same
cold, keeling streets as he had come on his tender whacked feet,
in his trip scuffed shoes with what he thought were the
remnants of his once keen mind, now glooping uselessly about

on the inside of his head. So he wandered slowly back by a different route to the narrow, four storey town house with the three deep grey, almost black, painted front doors. Moving at a clip with relief through to the other side of the middle of these, he slumped down in a crumpled sleeper on the floor of the hall.

Whatever it was that he and the mind peering medicine man had said to each and the other during their poorly head chats, the words might have been lost without meaning as Woller continued to leap out of a sleeper in the earliest hours, crash whirling his bones out of bed to fall in a smack against the wall, his lungs heaving to burst as he sucked in air through his rattling teeth. What seemed to be worse in his reckoning was that this sometimes happened when his eyes were wide open as well as when they were tight closed either for sleeping or for hiding, even when he was sat on a chair or stood by a window, looking out and feeling the hurt of a lurching spasm in his chest. At times seeing his hands but losing their sensation, all out of touch and balancing use. Stumbling on his own two feet, he felt as though they had been clumsily stitched or stuck on the ends of his weighted legs, each of which had the feel of nothing less than coarse stuffing forced roughly through the bursting of seams. And no matter how hard he punched with his fists at his own sack of bones, there was a hurt or an ache to be found needling hot and then cold and always around. He screamed without sound on the inside. While, on the outside, he pulled a gurning face at the mind cracking wither of hanging his own means on a frame of worn marrow. Woller attempted to walk off his frustration at what he was convinced was the jacking lack of the essence of a creative fink in a loose fit hole. With a haul on his whacked out knackered self and his coarsely stuffed legs, he took as much of the rest of him that would follow on from a push of his deadening feet tied down fast in his boots. Gone as he was, he booted off across the flat fields and through the running creeks along the wide cut drains. Under the tall trees which lined the sides of the lanes and arced high over his clomping and his sliding, his crashing and his tearing. Although he could not be sure where he was going, he thought it was something he ought to do in the vainest of hopes that something would come his way in a favourable turn. But with an apparent stopper of such, the further and harder at it he went the more it seemed as though his mind was having less than a reckoned idea about the how or the when of the matter being shifted to a soon gone covering over. One of long time looking out from the inside of his own thinking thoughts. And again, searching for the mattering means. Some of which was easier to imagine than to do. Well knowing that sooner and not later he would be wanting to be somewhere that was elsewhere, he said to his friends and those who knew him that he was keener than ever to be gone before he was talked out of it by them and their concern for narrowing bone. It was said by some that there was a need for a rest. A slowing down or a slight slackening off from all the hard booted slogging across each of the bare fens, breathing warm from the cold in the muffled wrapping of a big grey coat, buttoned high against the head cutting east wind. Then he said that if there *were* words to be spoken he would stand to one side of their meaning well on the matter with his fingers stuck tight in his ears. At least until each of them could see that whatever might be forecast could be so shot full of holes as to be worse than if it had not been seen at all. It was obvious enough to him in his own mind that he was filled up more than he needed to be with the thinking of others who knew less than much about him, sat back as they were on the fat of their own eloquent advice. Whether or not he ought to be wanting to bag up and boot his way back out to Algakirk in the northern fens so that he could make a serious attempt at knowing about being and doing both earlier than then and later than could be seen, was his concern he thought. In the event, he was minded to be going which he hoped would be a good thing. For him to find a way of his own would be a start. To be getting something which would allow him to clamber at will without recourse to a stinker of a pill to be taken at a happening moment of his gasping blink. This would be a thing to be had. And for which he was enthused to a point of excitable leaping, up and then down in his shoes while a grinning stretch of his lips appeared just under his nose, as he reached with a hand for his telephone with the intention of calling the mind peering medicine man to arrange an almost immediate consultation. Soon and short time after turning himself up on the edge of Algakirk, it began to occur to Woller that it could be not too much of a surprise when he thought he might be able to feel a sense of relief. Maybe this was because he was stronger in his boots and less than more cracked in his loose hanging bones than he had been before then – better he thought than he might have imagined. Although, if there were reasons or even a single reasonable explanation for this it was not one he knew. What he thought he *did* know was that such sudden come optimism of the sort that was sluicing through his brain ought to be sought for its uses in helping him take a hop and a jump straight down and in to the poorly head shrinking. At least while he was getting the good juice coursing through his veins as much as it was, enough that it might just knock on well toward his cracking mind for a final gone time. As he clomped along on his quickening step, he could see that he was making his way down one side of an old, part grassed, part dirt track that had the appearance of being a well used and familiar route for a shoe legger such as himself to get into and out of the village. When, in a flash, he jolted his bones to a sudden quick stop, he realised in a moment he had done so because he had forgotten to remember the *where of* and *in what* he would sleep. He stood where he was while he scratched at his head. And rubbed a hand across his chin. Eventually, he decided with a grump that there was little he could haul into his own recall on the matter of where and how he might heel off his shoes, when the sun eventually fell down over the side. It seemed as though he would have to find another pile of bricks elsewhere in Algakirk with a roof for him to bed crawl under if there was such a place to be found, he thought, with a ha and a hum. With a glance at his watch, he was pleased to see that he still had some of the afternoon light to be got through before it would become too dark and therefore, confusing to look for a house where he could put up his feet if only for a short time. In anticipation of a sustained mind rummaging process, he was well knowing that he would need a place with his own space where he could simply be without having to do much of anything at all except for a spell of long spent heel, kick waiting around for the next couched tilt at poorly head peering. It was fen stark and cold as he began to walk around the quiet lanes in search of a new, at least for the next while, home from home. There were fewer than he would have thought of the fennermarsh people to be seen out in the freezing air. Those who were had made a sense making choice of neck wrapped scarves and glove clapped hands to keep themselves warm as they did whatever it was they were doing before going into their houses when the moon became brighter than the sun. As he walked with what he hoped was a nonchalant demeanour in an attempt to appear less like a stranger, Woller was sunk down in his bones to see that in most of the windows of each of the houses he looked at there were lamps lighting up with a yellow bulbed glare, switched on by those inside. Their intentions, he assumed, were to fill with the glaring all of the rooms which could be seen from the outside. Continuing on around a corner, he was about to give up and roll himself down in a ditch or under a bush when he saw what he thought was just what he needed. Squatting four square and low at the end of a row of brick built piles of both wider and taller construction was a small, cream painted sort of a house that had the appearance when peered at, as he did, through the gathering dusk, of being as old as it was possible for a fennermarsh house to be. Woller stood out at the front of what he had decided would be his next while home, looking at what he could see of it in the spill of the neighbouring lights. He *could* see that it had been built for a fashion that had been a long time gone or maybe lost with the needs of its builder and their own choosing, whenever each had been. The slated roof was raised to a pitch at its centre where a single chimney, with a single chimney pot, sat like a hat on the top. And deep set into the front of the house was a wooden door painted a scarlet red. On either side of this were two small windows, smeared with grime too thick to be seen through from the outside. And quite likely, it would be the same from the inside too, thought Woller. As he walked around to the back, then back around to the sides, he realised there were no other windows or doors to be found or to be gone through which meant that the scarlet red door was his only choice for getting himself inside. And knowing this, he knew too without understanding how that the house was abandoned. It could, therefore, be open to a finker or more who might turn themselves up on its outside to wriggle a way in. Hum ha, he thought, reckoning that this time the finker or more would be him. Stepping up close to the scarlet painted door, he was about to reach out a hand so as to give the handle a twist when he was knocked back on his heels on seeing that where a handle ought really to have been, there was not one to be seen anywhere. There was no handle at the top or at the bottom or even at the sides in the frame. He stopped for a moment and stared at his hand as though it might be to blame for the handle being lost. With some annoyance he then kicked out with a shoe at the scarlet red painted door which sharp cracked on its hinges and flew wide open in a sneezer of fine dust, causing him to pull his scarf in a flash, up, over his nose and his mouth while he closed his eyes tight before blinking them open in the soon clearing air. Stepping further inside, he took a sniff for a keeler that would do him in quicker than he could move. There were, however, no smells there to be scared of and he eased his lungs back in his chest. As his eyes began to adjust, Woller was not much surprised to be looking at only one room, though he found himself more than a little bemused at how bare it was containing, as it did, nothing other than the accumulated worth of its neglect. Most of this appeared to be the dust among the cobwebs strung from the ceiling to the walls, to the windows and to the floor. With the light from outside almost gone, to the point where it was barely coming through the two small windows to where he was stood, he was minded to think there was little he could do in the gloom but lie down on the floor and wait for sleep. And so he did. The hitch to this, as he knew well, was that he had never seemed to be much of a sleeper on the floor wherever it or he might have been, being sooner and not later awake and staring out at the dark, wondering where the initial rush of his wanting to do along with his wanting to be seemed to have gone. Then whatever it was that had pulled him with a reasoning lack to follow whichever route held the promise of exciting new sights, sounds and tastes, would be turned belly up, sudden time quick with no hint of a warning, losing all purchase to a cutting run. It was, therefore, he suggested to his own self, not much of a surprise if he sank his mithering bones as hard and as sharp down on the floor as he could; as though he was laid there in the hope that he would push himself through to the ground beneath the small house where he might stay a while without a need for him to trouble expectation or for it to trouble him. The sticker was that he well enough knew just how much of a grump he would continue to be in as there was no way for him to avoid the sides of his own brain which were hard not to feel or to hear. And it was even more so then, when each of them sparked off a fizz and a zizz at the other, at a sounded pitch of a sort he had never heard before. Worse than this, the racketed difference in the ways to be gone from his minded jostling threw him off kilter with a reel of a hair tearing sort about which he was less than more sure how to call to a halt. In addition, he then took a slide to coming close on succumbing to an urge to pick up the telephone again, this time to hurl yelling words at the mind peering medicine man, to blame him for all he had said or to suggest that he claim some of the responsibility for the leaping slack and the dog down colour of gloom that was beginning to weigh in his brain. Woller could not find enough clarity of thinking to work out in his muddled, soft wrapped mind if he was actually there with the thoughts he was having or not. Caught as he was with the sudden come realisation that if he were to be a finker who would not disappear it might not be possible to know much about anything at all. And that he might sometimes have been right if he had not sometimes been wrong, according to the opinion of some. But for Woller, when he applied reason to the existence of his own matter he became more and not less bugged out bewildered, knowing as he did that there might be a sanctioned difference between the right thing and the wrong thing. And also, between the trivial and the profound. It was the notion of something being certain that scared him up frit, leaving him confused on the question of what he could do to move as close as he could with a clearer mind to make himself more than ever understood. Hum ha, he thought, as he fell into sleep. Waking, with the morning light streaming in through the deep set windows, Woller reckoned on getting a quick start to the day. And to be sooner than not stood in his sack of bones on the floor, legging it off through the scarlet painted door and out of the small, cream painted sort of house. He was, however, so filled with an ache, from his head to his feet that he stayed, laid where he was without moving much more than he deemed to be necessary. The cold seemed even starker than was usual for the eastern fen, causing him to pull his knees up, over and down on his chest, then to push his numbing hands into his armpits in a hopeful go at keeping himself warm. Outside in the lane, he could hear the sounds of people moving about doing the means to be done for the hour as it was. And as he listened with a more curious ear, it became clear that they were talking about how it was cold enough for snow which each and all of them predicted would fall much sooner than otherwise. Minded to think of the arrival of snow as a good thing, Woller decided to continue to lie as he was and do nothing else other than that until the cold enough matter began to drift onto the roof above him which it then did in small flakes that fell with a soft patting on the window panes not far from his head. Twisting his shoulders round, he thought he would lie in a lean in order to see what he could when in a leap out of nowhere that surprised even him, he was on his feet which were already shoed, to fumble with his hands at the lack of a handle on the scarlet painted door. In a moment, he had prized it wide open, rushed out, of the small, cream painted sort of house and hurtled off down the lane in the now swirling air. Coming to a stop with a barely heard crunch of his shoes on the snow beneath him, he stood as still as he could to listen with keening ears to whatever he might hear so far out of the village as he had come in the middle of nothing, as it seemed to be. With a ha hum, being just as he thought it would be, the only sound to be heard at that moment was the sound of his own breathing which cut through the quiet of the white covered fen, as he stood where he was. Listening and watching, he slowed to a barely pulsing beat as the slow warming yellows of the sun were beginning to fall across the fields where nothing could be seen to move through the now large whirling flakes, coming down thick and fast.

Stilled for a moment, he closed his eyes to feel as much as he could see with the little feeling he could summon into his bones, each of which seemed to be cracking in the freezing air. Reckoning he ought to try a loosening flail of his coat bundled wrapping he did so and could sooner than ever before feel his bones beginning to warm through, making sense of his arms and his legs and his hands and his feet. And his fingers and also his toes. Sudden time then with a bang to his brain, he was shaken with a needling urge to jump. To be jumping up and down in the falling snow, in an emptied lane, by a silently filling, wide cut drain seemed to him the only thing to do. And so he did, laughing and singing out words while losing his balance and the sense of it all in the arc of a leap, kicked as he was with a har de har of sudden come joy. When he then threw himself higher than before, he fell down, hard on a hip. Noo wah, he said, caught sharp with a hurting surge as he searched with his fingers for a crack or a smash of fragmented bone. There seemed to be no damage or obvious cracks, leaving him free to push himself up, back on to his feet again, noticing as he did so that he was starting to sweat through his clothes with the heat of his own need for a whirling hurl. Caring less, however, about this than continuing on, he slipped in a staggering run further along the vanishing track, his toes rubbing sore in what were now sodden shoes, to the top of a low bank where his sudden appearance seemed to startle a pair of black water fowl causing a splash, flapping burst of wings against wet reeds as the birds flew up and out of the dyke in a furious, honking fit. With a quick going thump, he watched them for a second or two then turned away and took off in a hurtling slide down the length of the bank, dipping his head against the slanting snow as he went, though what started out as a sliding hurtle became a scramble in the deepening drifts under the wires of the telegraph poles that were stretched out in a follow of a line, leading way off across the whitening fen to the horizon then gone from sight. After only a short distance, he was heaving a breather which was harder than ever to get down into his lungs, whacked out knackered and hurting sharp as he could feel them to be. And so he came to a stop in his sore making shoes. With a feeling ease to the hurt, he was pleased to stand where he was to wait for his chest to loosen a tightening hold and for his shoulders to widen their swing, when without even the smallest hint of a warning he thought about the meedler vong. Although he could not remember who it had been, someone, somewhere had talking told him about the searching berserkers who were known to appear in a flail of arms, legs and boots, loose from the reason of a questioning mind. Charging wide across the fen lands, across the fields, leaping over dykes, haring along the tops of the wide cut drains, through the running creeks of sucking mud, racing along the open lanes, down and around the streets of the towns, rushing, shrieking, pleading and yelling out for the meedler vong, each of them caught with needing to know, to understand something that had never been much understood, to be off in search of the meedler vong wherever it might be. Wondering then, he thought too about their recent time crashing in, on and through the still bewildered fennermarsh people who were caught with surprise to be found in Algakirk on the pointed end of a fingered poke, to be prodded, to be rough collar grabbed, to be begged and to be threatened in a hurl of yelling words for the whereabouts of the meedler vong. Although, as bad as it was in their telling words there were some who thought it could have been worse, for the berserkers had rushed at their search without considering the weight or the number of doors to be hit with a flail of their limbs or the cut of the claws on the cats that each of them ought to be screeching at. And because none of them were given much of a clue on the manner in which a snake might be charmed or a nod to a method for the hounding of dogs while pleading with crows that screamed with a haw before teasing them some more, there was less than most of a whack to be taken than there might otherwise have been. All of which served only to trigger a snap in the berserking brains of each and all of those who were looking madder than tops as they ran in a flap from a weighted door, to a clawing cat, to a waiting snake, to a howling dog, to a trunk of the crow held trees, fumbling for a lower grown branch up which they could climb to get at the teasers above. On finding nothing so low for the climbing to be done, the loopers took flight there and then with the heeling speed for which they were known, gone in a flash to be seen in shrinking size from the village as gawking, jerking figures, flitting along the top of the bank that ran down the length of the wide cut drain. And even though he could not be sure, it seemed to Woller that they would be gone for some time.

First published in Great Britain by Curious Press
www.thesocietyforcuriousthought.com

A catalogue record of this book is available from the British Library
ISBN: 978-0-9568280-0-2

Produced by Jacqueline Burns, www.londonwritersclub.com

Text and Cover Design by Two Associates

Printed and bound in Great Britain by MPG Biddles Ltd, King's Lynn, Norfolk, PE30 4LS

2 4 6 8 10 9 7 5 3 1